The Homed

a Love Story...

Eleanore Hill

Gingerbread Girl Press

Carpinteria CA

The Homed, a Love Story... © copyright 2016
Gingerbread Girl Press Eleanore Hill
ISBN 978-0-9970495-1-0

www.eleanorehill.com

The Marty Series by Eleanore Hill

The Family Secret: A Personal Account of Incest
The Last American Housewife
Period Pieces
The Gingerbread Girl
Corduroy Leopard

also
How to Cook for Your Dog
To Become a Landlady
In the Aftermath of an Overdose

Contents

chapter one

The beach lay out there, empty. Mavis parked, drawn to it this time of year. All the tourists, gone, 'summer lingering, not yet fall, the air still laden with warmth to bathe her longing flesh. This seaside town had betrayed her. A town she'd been born, married, and divorced in; and left languishing in. Mavis liked this time of year, the in-between seasons where seasons didn't show themselves. Palm trees never change anyway; the sand and sea unchanging. She liked the in-between times best; this time of the month when the moon was in its full cycle and she in hers, and she at the peak of hers when she was most passionate; she and the moon, waxing and waning; but she did not like this season of her life. Being in between youth and old age frightened her and left her confused. Would she go into old age alone, without love, without having babies? Where did the years go? What was she doing for forty- some years?

Mavis left her shoes in the car and made her way barefoot, her California soles toughened by years of running along the tide line. She pressed down the border of ice plant hard and cool, alighting on the still hot sand. Late afternoon, the in between day and night was the time she let go of the day before embracing the night by running. She ran along the tide line feeling the gentle foam slide up between her toes, bathe her feet before it retreated to gather forces and return to repeat this act. Playing on the edge of this large body of water was Mavis' joy. She breathed deeply, sweat sprouted on her forehead, soon to run down her neck between her breasts, counting on the sun, just above the trees to set behind the purple mountains, knowing it would miss them, and sink into the blue ocean, as she rounded the point, leaving its spectacular colors on the current. Guava, persimmon, apricot. This evening hues of lavender flooded the sky and water; last night it was flamingo pinks. Each sunset put on a splended show, as if for her alone. It was her beach, below the high tide line. She raced the sun every evening, knowing she'd win by reaching the pier before the sun touched the earth; that she'd see the fat, open, panting and naked anemones looking like vaginas around the shafts that held up the structure, waiting to be immersed again by wave upon wave of their lover the sea. Houses, businesses, cars, silouhettes of people were up above where civilization was taking place.

As she approached the point of the beach where the pier jutted out over the water, Mavis stopped to tighten her running bra, inhale deeply, stretch to touch her toes and release tension in the backs of her legs, looking upsidedown at the footprints she'd left in the sand, single file. Footprints with good arch markings and straight-ahead toes. No duck foot. It was one of the few good things her husband, Bill, used to say about her, "You walk with your feet straight ahead and your shoulders back." She'd never forgotten the compliment, nor his insults. To keep her under control, he used to put her down, and in those days it worked; it made her doubt herself. He told her that her nose was too long, her fingers too spidery; and her bare feet an embarrassment to him. He came from well-shod people with shorter, thicker, and blunter bodies and minds.

Mavis pants as she comes down from the run with the sunset splashing color on her auburn hair and freckled fair skin, catching her green eyes, as she enters the shadow cast by the pier. It will be a mile down and a mile back. The ocean air will push the busy boulevard pollution of traffic exhaust and fast food smells toward the mountains away from her. The constant fresh breeze coming off the ocean fills her chest. She takes deep breaths and lets them out slowly. This is why she has not left her little town. The beach is vital to her well-being. This beach in particular where she grew into a woman playing on the edge of this large body of water, leaving footprints in the sand, on a beach, a space no one owns where no one can tell you you can't be there. Where even the homeless have the right to be. It used to bother her that she and the homeless seemed to occupy the same space, this beach. The salty iodine air moves in and out of Mavis' chest, making it rise and fall. She closes her eyes to red pulsation and nothingness, and lets the evening mist bathe her face, the sand and water massage her feet. The sun has been swallowed up just under the surface of the horizon, sizzling as it sinks into the sea. The motion and rhythm of the breakers as they roll in and curl, soothe her. So close to the boulevard, yet so far away. The primordial sea rocks her in its cradle curve of coastline. Hot tears suddenly sting her eyes as she opens them. Alone. She feels utterly alone. Left alone. Left. Beyond love. How long has it been since she was held and kissed and been made love to. Since she has been loved. Her mouth turns down, quivering, as she tries to control it. Her face distorts and she can't hide her emotion. Can't lie. Has never been able to cry without looking like the mask of tragedy, a silent primal scream. Self-conscious, as if someone is in the dunes seeing her cry sobers her. The tide has washed away the sand at the waters edge in its ebbing and left the dry sand high. Mavis suddenly remembers the homeless again, perched in the dunes with their bottles. A lone one or in twos or threes. It's the lone ones she fears. The ones sitting, brooding together, with their desperate, bloodshot eyes, sandy hair, rag clothes, weathered in a way no male anywhere is weathered except peasants in desert countries, laugh and talk. Alone, they may be capable of taking out their misery on some passerby. Who knows if they hate women.

Narrowing her eyes, wiping the salty sweat and tears away, Mavis cuts it off in mid sob, scanning the high sands. She sees no one; it is completely deserted. She remembers being braver at a younger age. All through her twenties and thirties she ran on vacant beaches at low tide for miles without a thought of danger. in her early forties, a kind of self-protectiveness set in like glue and held her from her younger folly. It seemed to happen in her body, yet she justified it with her mind, thinking of all the stories on the news of violence; the world having been a saner place when she was younger, and other much-repeated phrases in the media. Two miles is all she'll go anymore. And along the boulevard in case she needs to run up and call for help. A concept that came after forty. Thoughts of predators.

Mavis settles her mind into a tranquility, dismissing the same old thought: I live on a post card, but am too small and dull anymore for the big job of taking in its beauty. Tonight she will simply be on it without dramatizing her situation. She wipes the sweat from her upper lip again and flips it onto the sand, squeezes her eyes shut to blink out the salty sweat from blinding her. Tonight the release of tension from sitting at her computer too long will be her goal; she'll walk a bit under the pier, and get beyond her brief show of grief over any and all of her losses, which have become the current emotionality since turning forty. Loss of love, beauty, youth, time, energy, whatever. Forty-three already, and nothing to show for it except a house and her career. Yes, the career was going well. Working at home now, for herself. That was a good move. Starting a graphic design business at home. At first she was afraid. It took time. She's built a reputation, acquired some important accounts on a regular basis; makes a decent living at it. Actually loves her work. And she does have a home. That's something, even if there is no prospect for love in sight. This could be it for her, beyond love, men, happiness. How'd she get so left out of everything she had always wanted in her personal life, and succeeded so well in her career? It baffles her every times she thinks of it and she can't shake the thought. It takes shape: she should have married Jim. If she'd known she'd end up with no one …. she'd probably have kids by now. He would have gotten a good job; a business major in college. They'd have a big house, a dog, probably a golden lab, drive a Volvo or one of those family utility vehicles, a Suburban maybe. She sees these housewives everywhere. They look smug, groomed to perfection, thin as teen-agers. They have it all. People treat women who have husbands and babies better, as if… As if they've done the right thing… But Jim drank too much, even though it was in college. Maybe he would have stopped…just a social drinker, a functioning alcoholic who wouldn't make a commitment. Ah, it wouldn't have worked out…Married Bill instead. The most miserable years of my life… but I got the house. At least I have a house, even if it is small…. the view makes up for it, overlooking her true love, the beach and the whole Pacific… Oh, men… Mavis puts it out of her mind. Men. There weren't any good ones. She made all the wrong decisions. This small seaside town didn't have any good choices in men to make. They weren't men, but aging boys, still playing, still hiking, biking, surfing, skateboarding, rollerblading, and drinking; still looking for hard-bellied beach babes, growing pots and pot of their own... She had to stop thinking about it or else she'd start feeling desperate, get that shortness of breath, be overcome by that feeling that life was a predator creeping up on her to get her. Uh, if I could only find a man.... That feeling that life was closing in on her, taking away her choices, squeezing her into that category of women they used to call old maids, spinsters. Well, she married; but nothing came of it...

Mavis neared the shadow of the pier contrasting to where the light of evening still lay on the sand. The sun, gone, taking the color from the earth, sky, and water. She crossed from the shade to light again, playing with the edge of each and stopped next to a creosote pylon, looking up at the great structure above her, feeling tiny, poking her bare toes into the anemones to see them close, and startled to the sound of a man's voice beside her on the sand. She looked down and there he was, lying beside a sprig of green, saying, "Beautiful! You're beautiful." Mavis pivoted to turn back and hurry away, when she heard him beckon to her, "Look, just look at this." She turned and looked. It was a tiny plant growing out of the sand in the debris left by the tide, among the tar, broken bits of styrofoam, seaweed, fish tackle, driftwood. The lonely part of Mavis responded to his voice. She stopped, walked back and looked closer. A tiny palm tree. From a date. A date palm. The once orange seed pod blackened by tar perched among the debris, rooted in the sand, still attached. "Isn't that a thing of beauty," he said. "Growing right here against all odds."

"Yes," Mavis nodded and looked directly at the man. He looked up into her face to see if she did, indeed, understand what he was saying. Mavis saw his eyes in the last of the light. Blue as the sea on a summer's day, set in a framework of hair the color of sand. Eyes and hair set off by the tan of his flesh which was sculpted and chiseled as if by erosion, a jagged rock beauty. He is Poseidon, she thought, a personification of the sea, sand and cliffs. A bone structure, hungered down to essence.

A man hungry in body and full in heart, she thought, and quickly snuffed the flickering of attraction out of her mind like the flame of a candle flaring up in the wrong place, while his visage took her breath away. Where was she? Confusion made her blink. What was a man of this kind of beauty doing under the pier? She wished to sketch him. His chin was upturned, sunbaked wide lips parted, white teeth barely visible, when he broke into a smile over her stunned expression. He reached up. "Hi, I'm Jack Spratt." Mavis wanted to laugh and say, You are? Grown up from the nursery rhyme?; but stammered her name, knowing better, "Mavis." He laughed. It's what most men did. An old-fashion name for someone her age. She was used to saying, "My mother was English," but said nothing to the perfect stranger. Perfect is right, she thought; and felt an arousal warm her belly. She reddened and stood there above him. He sat up from his leaning position and she saw how long and strong and lean his legs in those worn-out jeans were. No stomach at all, just a t-shirt stretched over a thin trunk, hugging broad lean shoulders. All bone, she thought; then raw bone. Then bone. That bone fleshed itself up in her mind's eye. Yes, she would sketch that, too. Later. She tried not to stare at his wiry arms, like intertwined snakes. It was a find, she mused. A rare find. She had discovered a beautiful man her age by appearances. Was this her real life or was she, indeed, in a painting of woman on a beach discovering a Greek God washed up after a shipwreck. Then she shamed herself. This was insane. A woman of her status doesn't talk to a homeless man. He is obviously a down-and-outer. He's been out in the weather, no sign of daily grooming. Mavis had an eye for this. Everyone did today. With one glance one could tell he had no home. But, she recalled, he'd given his full name. She turned to cast an eye out to sea, to see if there was the wreckage of a ship upon the reef off the mile buoy. A whimsy came over her and she said, with a teasing, playful lilt to her voice, "Jack Spratt could eat no fat and his wife could eat no lean and together they licked the platter clean…"

chapter two

A man with a nursery rhyme name and she, Mavis, a barren woman. She said "And he could eat no fat..." while she gazed on his bony structure. That was his opening. "Touché," and with one hefty laugh, got up and stood tall beside her, their shadows combined under the shadow of the pier.

"When I see something like that, I just have to talk to it," he pointed down to the tiny palm. She looked in the direction of his finger, nodded, suddenly shy, noting the length of his finger and the size of his hands. He's worked with those hands, she thought. And made love with them. Capable and graceful. The delicacy of his index finger pointing, like a ballet dancer's, like Moses' almost touching God's in the Sistine Chapel.

Again a stirring in her stomach, and a comparison forming. Jack had blunt square hands so thick and pulpy and hard he could hammer a nail with them, and did if one came loose in the wall of their home. Jack went on in that voice ushered out on his prominent Adam's apple, a male tone that soothed the female of her. A primordial male material, like the ocean speaking to the primordial female material she was made of, transcending the manmade details of daily living. Civilization was just turning on its night lights over there on the bouevard and she wasn't running for help, fearing a predator. Instead, she felt in the presence of protection. If Life were going to get her now, he would surely ward it off. The woman in her responding to the man. She inhaled his body scent. Male. Clean Male. No rot. Sun baked. Sand toasted, salt water-dripped and breeze-dried. She breathed him in and held the air of him inside her lungs quietly, exhaling when she could no longer contain him inside her. It had been so long. Years. Seven to be exact.

"It's hard enough to live, to stay alive, to make a go of it. To exist. You know." Was he telling her he was a bum, a drifter, a homeless man with those words? Was he embarrassed and explaining himself in this way. She heard only the deep melodic song. *From Here to Eternity*, that scene in the rushing tide. Lovers' passion.

Mavis pulled herself out of her stupor, making an effort to step aside and get control. He was no one to her. Was she so desperate? "Yes," she heard herself say, all business. "I know …" She paused, and then went on. "Well, I've got to run," and was about to sprint away. She knew his eyes were toying with her. She knew she'd never leave if she looked up and saw the twinkle. He loved this little plant because he identified with it, he's a survivor, too. Against all odds. The therapeutic clinical one was a no-nonsense part of Mavis. She's stayed too long with this man gushing over a one-inch palm that would be destroyed by the next high tide.

He said, "So long, then...." His breath entered her mouth and nose and she tasted him as he bent ever so slightly to talk to her face to face. He didn't smell of alcohol...it was of clean saliva, wood and leather. No, what was it? She tried to identify it. As clean as a horse's breath. Yes, that was it. She had caught the scent. Field fresh, fresh air fresh, and male. Again a snap comparison flashed on Jack's breath, uh. He'd been a smoker. The air from his lungs smelled rotten of decay.

The way Jack Spratt was able to dismiss her made her want to stay until he didn't want her to go. The way he said "So long," a polite manly farewell, triggered an impulse. She lingered, hesitating as if on the brink of an abyss.

"Do you want to run with me?" It was a foolish question, but since he'd detained her, it had turned night. The full moon was just rising. He'd figure she was afraid to run at night. She hugged herself against the damp sea air, suddenly chilled to the bone. Or was it emotions, the awful loneliness, and now opening herself up for rejection. His eyelashes lay sweetly downward as he studied her. She stepped back and viewed him viewing her proposition.

"Yes," and with an easy gait, they fell into a rhythm along the tideline with the tip of the moon just emerging from the solid night sea horizon, widened by the Earth's curve, as golden as a ripe pumpkin.

If she closed her eyes, she could have mistaken his gentle comments for an educated gentleman's, not a homeless drifter's, as they jogged the mile back and then walked up through the deep cool sand, side by side to her car parked along the boulevard. They were back to civilization with a tiny beach cafe winking its coffee house lights at them, beckoning to them, luring them with its exotic aromas. A Clean Well-Lighted Place it was called. She had been there many times. Alone, over a cup. Reading. As she brushed the sand from her feet, leaning against her car, she felt his hesitation to leave her.

He stood, awkward, for a moment, and then gestured toward the cafe. "Will you come have coffee?"

Mavis nodded. A mere puppet tonight, on strings, lower jaw dropping, coming unhinged, ready to say, "Uh, huh," to any request he made.

He shifted from one Li'l Abner-long denimed leg to another. "You won't be embarrassed being seen with me?" Mavis laughed and looked into his eyes and saw a humbleness there. He meant it. He knew his place and hers. A certain embarrassment had entered his bearing, since their run. She was of another world, and he was on the periphery of it and did not want to be caught trespassing. He was as vulnerable as she. To be rejected by a homeless after opening yourself up would be an all-time low for her; and for her to reject him would confirm his status, which he had dealt with by avoiding people with houses and cars for how long now? He's ashamed, she thought. Her heart went out to him. It's not false humility, she thought. I've made him feel shabby. She pulled at her bright t-shirt and tights, as if to press them away out of sight. How pretentious, after all, this cerise jogging outfit is. She suddenly felt conspicuous, knowing how much all the fluff she wore stood out, while he blended into the landscape. They began to walk toward the cafe.

They found a table out of the draft of the doorway. She sat down, listening to the espresso machine making the sound of a jet taking off, while he made his way between the art deco tables and ordered two teas from the young guy with the dyed hair and eyebrow, nose, ear and tongue rings, behind the counter. She had given up coffee. She watched Jack Spratt amble over, stand on one foot and then the other, a tall guy in old jeans and tee, reach into his pocked and put a bunch of coins on the counter. She saw this but heard nothing over the noise of the espresso machines. She never went on her runs with a puirse of any kind, had no money on her, herself. This could be humiliating. He probably didn't have enough to pay; but as soon as the thought was out, he turned, carrying two steaming mugs, with that wide white smile and the eyes with the twinkle. All his wealth was in his flesh, she thought. Bill, the comparison flashed. Uh, a big wallet full of money, but uh. He'd gone to pot. All that ice cream he liked to eat when he tried to give up smoking...

Mavis would ask the age-old question, but in reverse. When he sat down, she said, "What's a man like you doing in a place like that. You know, under the pier?" He laughed and his magnificent Adam's apple covered all over with that delicious ruddy gooseflesh protruded. Did the male neck contain such a protrusion to attract the female? Was it a small erection, that thing in his throat, to hint of greater things below. Again the warmth of arousal flushed through her body.

They talked into the night; but the words were meaningless. Mavis couldn't remember later what they'd said to each other. Coffee drinkers came and went, the noise of chatter all around them provided a backdrop for their own performance. When the pierced young man began blowing out tall candles and flicking the lights, stacking the wooden chairs on the tables, and sweeping the floor, they came back long enough to realize that hours had passed without their being aware of it. The place closed at midnight. The moon was high in the sky, smaller and cooler than its hot emergings, unlike they themselves. They were flushed and heated and swollen with exchanging words, reaching the other's mind. Their bodies were ready to explore as an extension of the mental intercourse. It had always been that way with Mavis. Until she reached a man's mind, her body remained closed. And now, and now... he had revealed his beauty of thought, had filled her with his words. A certain weakness was in her knees and elbows. She had lost her runner muscles, as she got up from the table. She could have swooned, stumbled, been picked up off the floor by him, so soft and female she had become.

With a carelessness almost a swagger that drifted up from her toes to her throat, Mavis invited Jack Spratt home, as he held the car door open for her. The words slipped out, from deep in her throat, as if the sultry one waiting inside her was tired of waiting and would no longer be put off, reckless beyond reason now. Again, Mavis stood on the edge of the abyss, testing her footing, tempting fate. Jack didn't answer. He just nodded, closed her door and went around to get in the other side. The light of the full moon bathed him. She reached across to unlock the handle, seeing him about to enter her private territory tinged in the gold.

Some other communication beneath words had kept them sitting over empty cups, having asked for more hot water, dousing their one tea bag between them. He'd bought one tea and asked for two cups and all the hot water they could drink. Was that how the homeless did it? They sipped until the hot water ran clear and they themselves, were floating. Neither had excused themselves for relief, riveted as they had been with the easy way they found themselves being together; so it occurred to each of them that they were bursting and had begun laughing over that state of physical numbing discovery can cause.

On the way to the car, with the cafe locked up, Jack had excused himself and disappeared behind a tall eugenia hedge. Mavis felt silly squatting down with the full moon risen overhead, a glorious gold ball, sailing in its own sea and casting its reflection on everything below, while she waited for a man she didn't know to finish relieving himself. She peed on her bare foot.

He appeared, adjusting himself and smiled, looking down at her, it seemed for reassurance. He asked, "Are you sure you want this, for me to come home with you?"

His legs were too long forr her little car. It amused her that even with the seat shot back as he released the lever, his knees still pressed into the dashboard. He positioned himself like a grasshopper wedged into a matchbox while she drove, glancing over or watching him from her side vision, and he told her this was the first car ride he'd had in about three months. She thought, he doesn't hitchhike?

chapter three

As they pulled into her driveway,' Mavis heard Jack exhale, long and audible, through his nose, and shift his shoulders as though the discomfort was not only in his cramped body. She feared that he may be doubting his manhood withher driving, her bringing him to her house, using him for his maleness; that he may not be man enough for her expectations, that he was not big enough for her, as big as a man ought to be. Not an important man. Was he a throw away man. Just a fuck. He had no job. She was in charge. She was the aggressor. Was she carting him home like so much cargo or just junk she'd picked up at a yard sale. Or a big overgrown stray dog. Did he think she felt sorry for him. Had compassion for his situation? Yet, at the same time, she knew that he knew why she had asked him to come home with her. Had it been so transparent. Her attraction to him and her lonliness, her desperation to have him. To have a man. To have someone. The silence between them, as she turned off the key and headlights, filled their ears. So this is where she lives, Mavis could almost hear him say. Nice view. Look at that moon. But, no word was spoken. In a kind of obedience, he followed her cue. She opened her door, so he opened his. They let themselves out of the little car; and without a word, he followed her down the little path that led to her house from the driveway. As they made their way carefully, using the light of the moon which was at the peak of its own path, before making its way down, they stopped to look at the radiant vastness of the sky and sea. She felt him beside her, could inhale his deep, hot breath on the air, while the moon seemed to stand still, as if to watch what would come next, casting the ocean into a million shards of gold mirrors; the glassy surface shattered into a restless current as the temperature dropped, shuddering like a horse's withers with the kiss of the wind.

Mavis turned to look at Jack as he looked at the splendor before them. This view was her first offering. As she turned, he was waiting for her with the moonlight in his eyes giving them the glint of steel for the moment it took for him to see her face illuminated in the moon's glow, and cupped her face in his hands and bent to touch his lips on hers. That reckless careless wanton female in her returned his kiss, wrapping her arms around this neck and embracing what, she knew, was forbidden fruit. He stood up straight and she came with him off the ground, and he held her there against him. Beneath vision warmth flooded her body. She hung limp from his neck wanting to to wrap her legs around his groin. There was no more waiting. Mavis gave herself up to him, a man who loved a palm tree in its infancy trying to grow against all odds. It was enough. A nice man. A delicious man. And, yes, a man who responded to her. Their silouhette danced in the moonlight as one figure. They went down on the path, dizzy with touching, shedding clothes without notice, kissing long and deep, unable to pull away, connecting with every inch of flesh they could, and when he pierced her body she wailed in sweet agony like a she wolf to the moon, for the pleasure of it, groaning and crying and rocking with him until they were spent. Neighboring dogs set off by her cry started up a cacophany of barking. By the time they lay back breathing deep, weak, laughing over all the noise they created, with her head on his arm, on their backs, her legs over him, limp and heavy against each other, the moon was gone, having nodded approval at its apex, curiosity as satisfied as their own, and disappeared into the sea, taking with it all the glitter it had shed on its night travels. How many hours had the moon been swinging in the sky watching. They lay in the dark on the path, naked, and began to laugh again, a magical laughter. Joy, pure joy was the sound that emanated. Mavis looked at Jack's face, propping herself up on one elbow and saw that his eyes were closed.

They flickered open and captured the only existing light, only her little porch lamp at the end of the path. She could feel her own smile stretch across her face. A real smile. She had not smiled for a long time; and now she couldn't stop. He reached up and touched her cheek with his magical finger tips, as if she were precious, as if he wanted to see if she were real. And, for the first time in a long time she felt real. Felt connected. Felt that she was where she wanted to be. The searching over and done with.

"Oow!" Her own voice returned to her, playful, finally feeling the earth beneath her elbow. He echoed, "Oow," and made the motions of getting his bare hindquarters up off the ground where pebbles had dug into his flesh leaving their marks. Was there some anesthesia that comes over lovers so they feel no pain? If passion is strong enough could lovers roll around in a briar patch and feel only the wonders of their love making, so lost in each other? Mavis got to her feet first, standing naked, while he lay there looking up at her and then took her cue. "l live outdoors," he murmurs in her ear. "This is fine. I don't have to go inside. l'll walk back. lt's warm tonight." She pulls him along, opens the front door and tugs him indoors, into her home. They stand there naked, holding their clothes in their hands, at the entrance of where she does her living, looking at her living room. She fills with pride for all she can provide. He nods, saying, "A very pretty place," bowing respectfully, then looks at her, smiles that broad white smile, with a twinkle of mirth in his eye, adding, "So, you are the homed. Oh, you homed ones! So, this is home."

She leads him by the hand through the house, room by room, so in the dark as they sleep he will have his bearings, in case he gets up. He whistles low, sometimes, and acknowledges each room with a nod of his head. The bright greens, yellows, fushia, and lavenders, splashed on couches, walls, beds, and floors. A very clean and well-lighted place she had created on her own and wants now to share with him. She sees him seeing the care and thought she's put into her home, the playfulness and fun she's had with decor, and it pleases her because it pleases him. His eyes lay long upon her computer until she furnishes him with a simple explanation, that of being a graphic artist. She strokes his chiseled jaw line, running her fingers down his hard chest, circling his groin and cupping his testicles in her palm, to illustrate how she sees line, symmetry and form. She catches an almost sheepishness in his manner and expression, as if he ought not be here; so she persists, dragging him, finally into the master bedroom, pointing to the bathroom, and leaves him there with a fresh towel, the biggest and thickest one she can find. She herself, likes small, rough, thin towels, thin enough to dry the inside of her ears with. For guests, its always the big ones. As she goes to the smaller bathroom, she glances back and sees him watching her in the polished mirrors, holding the towel with one large hand over his privacy. He winks. She blushes, and hides behind closed door to repair herself.

Mavis crawls into bed first, listening to the sounds Jack makes behind his door. Water running, flushing, splashing, then silence. He emerges in the flesh, walking toward her, as she gazes upon his exquisite nudity before he joins her.

chapter four

Mavis wakes first and doesn't move anything but her eyes. She wants to see Jack sleeping. Careful not to wake him, she gazes across from her pillow; and there is his sleeping face. The visage takes her breath away. Where there was no one there is now such a being. Such a fine beautiful male human being in broad daylight. A man. The words form for the first time: He's a man. She knows what it means now. It occurs to her that she has never had a man before, just boys and then older boys and then old boys. Or is man. Is he a god she found washed up on the beach last night, and she, suddenly, turned fair maiden? Carefully she lifts her head from the pillow and views the comforter to see the form he makes in her bed, a large mound or flat, or what. She expected he would make the comforter into a big mound, but sees it's flat as if no one is under it. She's as playful and curious about this new creature as a kid, wanting to explore him from all angles; and spies his feet sticking out at the end of her bed. Her throat tightens in the delight of it, a man too long for her bed. She studies his toes. Each one perfect, long, symmetrical; each feature matched by her immediate comparison with Bill. Why does she still use Bill as a reference point. It annoys her as she recalls his thick stubby toes with nails like claws that had to be cut with a special scissors. Mavis sees that Jack sleeps on his back, squared off, "like a man"; and wonders when she adopted these manliness standards, as the words come: "fearless, baring his neck, vulnerable." Bill always curled up in a fetal position, mouth agape like a fish out of water with a belabored esophagus. And he hogged the bed, never aware she existed once asleep, snorting into the pillow like a hog after truffles. But, Jack. How does he know how to be the right way, sleeping with his mouth closed, clean breath coming in through clear nostrils, the way she thought a man would sleep. No snaggles as if about to strangle; no whistling. No phleghm. A very clean man. He's the one, Mavis almost said aloud, that I've wanted to meet all my life. He's the one I pictured in my fantasies. He's the template in sepia. He is here now; and peace filled her.

Without waking him, she slips quietly out of bed, goes to the far bathroom and takes a robe off the door hook and slips into it and hurries to the kitchen, not wanting to wash off his fluids dried on her, or his smell, closing the bedroom door against any noise she may make. She hums as she grinds the gourmet beans for coffee and, takes down two blue mugs to receive the steaming brew; no tea this morning. She readies the espresso machine, while listening to any sign of life in the bedroom. A light goes on, and she hears the shower and then the sound of her electric razor. A pan of tofu vegie omelet is coddling on the burner with whole wheat bagels warming in the toaster, at the sound of the door opening. She is placing fresh organic mangoes on the fruit dish. She wants to see how he eats a mango; and already knows; but wants to confirm it. She knows so much about him now, by just being with him. When she turns to see him in the doorway of the hall, steaming, wearing a towel around his loins, torso tapering up naked to his fine flat hard and sparsely haired chest, just enough hair around flat nipples, she pretends she's all business, suppressing the urge to play the fool and throw herself upon him again. The automatic contrast to Bill distracts her. He began growing breasts when he gained weight, like a hermaphrodite, had fur like a bear which hid his teats. Women were not the only ones whose nipples revealed arousal and readiness. Most men didn't know this; but Jack knew how excited she was last night when her nipples were visible through her t-shirt. She felt her nipples harden and stand erect as they'd talked and Jack's eyes hadn't missed a cue. Now, Mavis feasted her eyes on Jack, while Jack entered her domestic scene, came to her and bent down and took her chin with one hand, turned her face up and met her eyes on her level. He studied them. The woman of them. The person she was. "Hello," he said. She said, "Hi," blushed, her face hot, and continued to gaze, suspended again in that other world. "We're a Far Side...," she said finally, breaking out of the spell he cast upon her. He kissed the last word to leave her lips, and she said it when he came up for air, "card." He knew what she meant, and he laughed, quoting a Far Side card, "They looked eyes from across the room." She wondered how homeless men know about cards. Do they go into stores and browse, too?

Then the hungry man, the stray dogtof him, came alive, sniffing the air with his fine prominent nose, flaired nostrils attuned, following his sense of smell to the stove. "Ummm," and glancing at the coffee, "Ohhh," and then at her again, "Ahhhh." They filled their plates, took their cups, and he strolled out onto the deck on the ocean side, seeking the outdoors.

Mavis followed behind him, basking in the sight of the back of him, studying his narrow hips draped in her thin rough small towel. Long straight legs below and tapering up above into broad lean shoulders, all golden. A walking man he was with a workman's musculature. Not gym muscles. Bill had bloated up at Nautilus, but turned to flab when he quit and looked like a peeled shrimp naked, speckled with moles and stretch marks across his lower back. Mavis marvelled at Jack's good skin, no blemishes, no fat, no love handles, and thought, a rolling stone gathers no moss. She shamed herself and wondered if he'd turn into a couch potato if he settled down, but knew better; he wouldn't let himself go to pot, and he wouldn't settle down. She couldn't picture him a slob. There was something about him. She surveyed her new lover, and let the question surface: why hasn't a woman captured him yet? How has he remained single? No divorces, no children, nothing left in his wake or a relationship history, unless he's not telling. 'Well, it's too soon to pry. And -a fleeting worry took ahold of her, leaving her shaken and helpless, as she chose the lesser of the chairs, an old aluminum deck chair at the patio table in her mismatch of deck furniture, leaving Jack the director's canvas chair. After all, he is heavier. She eyed him in the morning sunshine, and feared she could not keep him, even though he'd murmured last night that he hadn't found his true love but hadn't given up. Was it just a line? He seemed sincere, in fact naïve to say a thing like that. A romantic. is that why he'd never settled down? No reason to. Still looking for his princess. He certainly could be cast by Hollywood as a prince charming. Did he carry a glass slipper in his hip pocket? Would it fit her tough California bare foot? He turned, silhouetted in the sunlight, an apparition descending from the heavens, she thought; and shamed herself again. She knew better than to do this, idealize anyone, let alone a stranger, a man, an indigent male. A drifter, a roamer. A world traveler, to be more generous. Is that what he was, a tumble weed, and she a morning glory vine, rooted in one spot that had temporarily intertwined with his briars. With a strong wind, he'd tear out her heart tugging at her roots, and move on. He interrupts her reverie. "It's a warm and friendly place. It's beautiful, just like you. Your home looks like you."

They sit on the deck with their feet propped and resting on the railing, steaming cups under their noses, and grin. All they have to do is to look into each other's eyes or just look at the other, and the grins begin, remembering how it was last night. His pride in bringing out her passion; her joy in finally having someone release it from her. They hardly got through breakfast seeing the other and growing warm all over again, swollen and wet. She saw that he was ready and smiled in sympathy for both of them. Through the scrambled tofu and her apricot preserves and seven-grain bagels, they merely hummed, taking their eyes off the other long enough to see where the food was, drenched by the presence of the other. She finally leaned back, brushed her lips with the back of her hand for a napkin, and felt sex coarsing through her blood. What was happening to her. Whatever it was, she was high on it.

After breakfast, Mavis goes in and brings out the bowl of mangos, holding it in front of Jack with a knowing look. He reads her tittilated hint, takes one and without breaking eye contact, holds the mango up to his mouth, salutes her with it and bites in, gently tearing away the tough outer peel in lover's nibbles, and, once baring the ripe red underflesh, sinking his lips, teeth and tongue into its sweet, juice, licking and sucking, gulping mouthfulls, letting it run down his chin, until mango is all around his mouth and dripping down his chest. Still pinning Mavis with eye contact, Jack reaches up to Mavis and smears mango on her and then cleans it off with his tongue, inviting her to wallow with him as she tastes the hard bone of his nose as he rubs his face all over her, down her neck, breasts, and putting it again into her swollen mouth. She thinks, yes, the lips swell, too, just like the labia, in love-making, and tries to stay without thought, without reflection, without knowing she has not swollen for a man for a long time. She grows weak in the knees and sits down in her aluminum chair, panting, watching as he wipes juice off his face at the last with the back of one hand and rubs it on his chest. She recalls an old movie where Jeff Chandler does that playing an Indian. The same gesture. Jack has used no knife, fork, spoon or napkin. Mavis has never felt so succulent. Then he throws back his head, baring his ruddy neck with its exquisite texture of testicles, the rough, goose-fleshed stretching, revealing the chiseled jaw line, a mere crag, and chuckles. She watches his Adam's apple bob, the wide white smile with the sunbaked lips, and is on fire with his having known what she wanted of him. He holds her with his eyes, rises, comes to her, takes her chin with one mighty paw, and licks her face, all around her mouth, nose, eyes, and sucks her tongue and then stands there, pulling the towel from his waist, so she can feel his member warm and smooth on her cheek, opens her eyes and there he is, his startling erection, petting her with it. It? What else to call it? He brushes it, gaining heat across her lips, eyelids, caressing, teasing her with such a helpless look. Oh, baby, is on his face as he keeps perfect timing to her arousal, answering her moaning, groaning each time and rubbing his heat down her neck, gently parting her robe, encircling each nipple with the tip of it, leaving a damp trail of lubricant, which makes her nipples stay as hard as he is. He stands astride her and leans in to perform with his magnificent instrument, while she opens wide, wet, helpless, ready. He enters matching moan for moan and stays against her without moving so he will last until she begs him to move. "Move," she moans. "Move....please move." And then he begins thrusting, half kneeling, the chair rocking, so he has to hold onto the arms of this aluminum chair to stabilize it, while she grabs his pelvic bones at the hips and pulls him in and in and in to her to his thrusting. The chair begins to lean and collapses as they groan and then shout together, falling to the deck, hitting the floor in orgasms, rolling around, locked together, bone, flesh, soul, until their cries can be heard far away, carried by the wind to the sea. They lay there as they had last night, laughing and weak over their accomplishment. Do the seagulls startle as their eroticism echoes as far as sound waves travel? Do they take to the air? One did, from the deck railing. It had come to beg for food. "Oh, it's good. So, so good." Her voice is a whisper.

"Getting laid," is what her best friend would call it. "Oh, so you finally got laid, ha, ha. It's about time. You were becoming a royal pain in the ass, you know." Mavis could hear her friend's voice as feedback to her thoughts. She argued in silence with the voice. But this isn't getting laid. This is, is... She couldn't think of the word. This is, uh, a trip to the moon. She laughed out loud and Jack cocked another eyebrow. Now Mavis understood the lyrics to the song.

Once again spent, Jack reaches up to snatch the flat, yellow, hairy, wet mango seed from the table, flops down beside her and places it on his tongue and lies like a baby, sucking on it, until Mavis laughs and laughs, weaker than she has ever felt. She pumps the air from her lungs in little spurts as he clowns for her in mock sensuality. He knew so well what she was onto. Telepathy, or just a man, a real man, a sensual man, sexy beyond belief, knowing what a woman wants. Needs!

Mavis has no bones. She is mush. She is the mango meat inside him. She is his, completely. The word "submit" rises in her mind. Ah, sweet submission. is this what it means. Unprotected now, without resistance, she lies there, his. And feels no fear. All instincts connect her to him; her will is his will, her flesh, his flesh, her soul, his soul. Eartha Kitt. She begins to hum, "What a difference a day makes...Twenty-four little hours, with sunshine and flowers where there used to be rain .... He exhales through his magnificent stallion nostrils, long and audible, and she inhales the clean sunshine male scent, and keeps this rhythym with her breathing, so she can keep him inside her. Pheromones. She began ingesting him the night before willingly. And now he has inoculated her completely, with his voice implanted in her, his smell, semen, taste, touch. Her brain is reeling with his body chemistry.

She thinks out loud, "They say you incorporate your lover into your body and your immune system recognizes it and you are a part of another person and they you. You are now coursing through my blood stream and I through yours. it's the same as putting data in the computer. You are now in my hard drive." Again the gentle chuckle, a glitter of mirth in the sky blue eyes reflecting daylight, so different from the steel blue in the moonlight, eyes like chameleon, changing with the light, as he puts his arms behind his head, shoves the broken aluminum chaise lounge chair aside. His underarm hair sprays out in a fan catching the sunlight. The sudden jutting of this male hair, exuding its humus, darker than the sandy hair on his head, sends a jolt through her groin. He could take her again, right now—she gazes, sitting up to get a full view of both armpits, picturing how to capture this in art form later. Ah, is there no end to the beauty of him. And wishes to paint him and photograph him, and graphic art him, and somehow, keep him and have him and love him forever. How could she ever survive it—he got up and walked out the door, saying, "Thanks, Bye." Her woman's heart, now that he has made her a real woman, knows that this male can not just walk away; that he meant it. Whatever it was, that he did to her, that they did together. That one doesn't have the capacity to just leave and never look back after this. How often does a thing like this happen between two people. It wasn't just fucking. They were making love. Love!

The sun moved overhead, found them behind the railing on the deck, blinded them, burned them, and finally chased them into the cool interior of her home. They went naked, flopping on the couch, entangling legs, foot to foot, each leaning against opposite arm rests, still wet and sticky from loving. Mavis leaned with every cell of her body heaving against whatever surface she touched. Gravity tugged her to stay, not move, anesthetized by sperm. A mere fly to a spider. She lay still, listening to her heart beat deep and slow, feeling it in her throat. Heart throb! She laughed and he cocked an eyebrow. Only a thought, not to be spoken. Too silly, girlish, teenage. Mavis drifted in the post-coital state, basking in the receding juices that had reached their height, flooding her system, and now, the storm over, trickled meekly back to the small streams they had been. She experienced this trickle of real fluid as his juices oozed out of her onto the good couch fabric, feebly attempted to get up and find a towel, but let the moisture lay there and soak in and stain her couch permanently, and leave traces behind for others to beware of. Precious moisture. She wanted to save it. She would never be the same; and other visitors to her home would twitch their noses beyond consciousness, picking up the pheromones of his presence. It tickled her/ as they slept, curling up, bottom to bottom, Mavis smiling ever so imperceptibly, waking now and then to view him, his great head upon one of her throw pillows, easy in the world of dreams, like the god he was, descended to earth, eyes laying softly closed with the lashes splashed downward just above the faint shadows of his cheek bones. When the shadows were long on the deck, and the last rays of sunlight slanted in through her glass doors in great yellow streaks, they roused, stretched and gazed upon eachother.

Jack moved first, stretching over and kissed Mavis, smiling and winking, and when she kissed him back, he carried her into the bedroom, where they were locked together again, clinging, moving, endlessly groaning again into the midafternoon summer air. And then they slept. When they awoke it was four p.m., and they began nuzzling and making love again, drunk on eachother. Then they got up to pee, to drink water, to grab fruit from the bowl, and came back to bed for more and more of eachother. When night came they slept, woke, had sex, slept again, woke, made love. By midnight they lay there entwined and spent. Without moving their heads, they looked across the tumble of bedding with only their eyes. The moon had been peeking in the window for hours throwing gold upon their nude sensual thrashing, highlighting and shadowing their lover's holds, like wrestlers among the bedclothes. In the remaining moonlight she could see the surfaces of his face.

It was serene, as if he were a man on a mountain top, having reached the peak; made it and now surveying where he had been, all that lay below. She felt kittenish, all squirmy and comfortable, never wanting to move off the bed, EVER. With great effort, Mavis switched on the bedside lamp.

"That was day one!" she ventured, but he only grunted. This was what was wrong with casual sex, she thought. She had read too much nonsense about multiple partners during her celibacy. Now he'll leave; I'll never see him again; all these. feelings, what of all the feelings I have, or could have for him. Where will they go when he's gone. She knew only too well that they'd back up, clog her system, and she'd feel the pain of withdrawal from love, drained and empty. All the sex chemicals leaving her, and worse, the one who induced it, not caring enough to stay. To stay around. To be her mate. "How silly," she chastised herself. It was only what it was, what her best friend Sue, would say, she got laid. And her friend would be right. That's all, after all, she'd picked him up under the pier. He was only a drifter. It wasn't like getting rejected by a respectable man. Mavis shamed herself. She'd just used him, then, just for sex. She was the disgusting one, then. While these thoughts tormented her in the aftermath of the triathlon lovemaking, on the ground, in the chair, floor, couch, and bed, he rose on one elbow and came to her with his gorgeous face and said, "I care about you. It's not just sex. You're a beautiful person."

"Oh, my," she thought. Does he read minds. Does he think I'm a teenage girl, or what? Is he telepathic or psychic. Or just intuitive. She just looked into his eyes for a split second and then impulsively pushed herself up and away from him, put on a t-shirt and tights, still not wanting to rinse his sex fluids off her skin, turned to him and said, "What do you want to eat. I've got food. Lots of it." He came to her naked, striding up with a serious face. "No, I mean it. You are a very special woman." Mavis simply continued, "Meat and potatoes or fish and rice?" He turned red in the face, "Meat. Hot and juicy," then sat on the edge of the bed and sighed, as if defeated.

chapter five

They get to know each other now that they've spent their physical passion, although it lays in wait, smoldering, ready to burst into flame, ignited by the other's presence. Like a couple of mating tigers, panting after sixteen hours of copulation, they sit around resting, gaining strength, until desire takes over again, and talk. Mavis learns Jack's personal history, a story live with enough detail to bring tears if she were the type. But, she isn't one to cry over the past; anyone's. She simply calculates the detail while he paints the picture, putting good description into her as if she's her computer, now that they're upright and in their minds. She translates his words as his understanding, delights in his articulation and insightfulness. Now she knows why he drifts, can't or won't let himself belong to any given place or person, never having wanted into the mainstream. She's read about peripheral people. Nomads emotionally. They cannot attach to one place or person in case of drought. They fear staying in one place too long, don't trust it. They're survivors who brush up against mainstream society but keep their distance. They are not hermits. They like to see what's going on, just not to participate in it. And they're incurable. She read something, or there was a documentary on 60 Minutes or something; she can't remember. Wasn't paying attention at the time; but now recalls the whole profile of this type of person. She remembers the words: set in their ways, fixed, loners to be sure. People who view others, live vicariously, love their freedom and spontaneity, love having no roots, love not knowing what's ahead. And, ah, now it's coming back in full, she remembers the commentator stressed that these drifters are tremendously resourceful in any situation except for belonging and joining.

Mavis knows her thoughts are running rampant and are glib. As Jack talks of his childhood in Idaho, a stepfather who beat him and his mother then died an early death of alcoholism; his mother moving into a trailer and taking up with one more drinker who treated her okay, but she died of cancer soon after that. She never wanted to return to the Reservation; She was full-blooded Nezperce, named by the French for their big pierced noses. Her people made her feeled soiled by the kind of men she chose. They figured she married the enemy. Indians in my grandmother's day were sent to American school so they'd give up their heritage. They didn't know how to raise their own kids as Indians. Any sign of hanging onto traditional heritage was frowned upon by the whites. It turned out they couldn't identify with either culture in the end. The white kids looked down on them, and they didn't know how to be Indians so they didn't fit anywhere. If they married within the tribe, they at least had that; but anyone marrying outside their own people had a real problem. She seemed to like blue-eyed, fun-loving government-funded workers that came out to handle Indian business. They always turned on her after awhile and called her a "squaw" and mistreated her. When she died, there was no reason for Jack to hang around the trailer so he hit the road at fourteen. He hitchhiked a ride to California by truck. Jack smiled, remembering all those truckers with fondness and how they fed him, tried to mentor him, talked on their radios about him. His code name was LLH for Long, Lean, and Hungry. They passed him from truck to truck to get him to California, as if he were their favorite son; tried to take him home to their wives or girlfriends; but Jack stayed clear of getting close to anyone; took odd jobs, went into the Seabees in San Diego at sixteen, lying about his age; he was tall; drove truck when he got out; and then got tired of being on the road and decided to sit around the beach, work when he had to just to get by. He read a lot. The library was free; the best thing that ever happened to America, he laughed. He had one good teacher in school who turned him onto books and believed in him; told him he had a lot on the ball, a good brain and all that and tried to get him into a foster home; but Jack wouldn't leave his mother with the men she'd choose. When his mother died he had no relatives to go to. Her people considered him a half-breed. His mother kept no connection to her own family. He'd never met anyone on either side of the family. There was no family member to come to the rescue who wanted to take him in. No one. Well, his biological father who left right after he was born, married a white woman and started another family. Just left the "squaw" with a newborn "half-breed," took off with a woman he considered his equal. She used to tell me things about him. He was a tall blonde man of Swedish and English descent, and about the most gorgeous man she'd ever seen driving up in a big shiny car. He had dealings with a housing project on the Reservation. He'd met this biological father once, right after he went off on his own. Looked him up. His mother had some papers in a jewelry box which he rifled through to see if there was anything of value. He found his father's name and an old California address. It gave him enough to go on.

The guy was sort of embarrassed to see Jack at his front door in a respectable neighborhood, knew who he was right away, stared at first and then recovered and told him he looked just like his mother, same features and color. He clearly didn't want to spend any time with Jack. He was a CEO of some big real estate corporation. He had a big house, a big car, a big family, and came outside so his wife couldn't overhear anything. He'd gotten a look at her, standing in the background, looking to see who rang. Blonde, well-dressed, the kind that require a lot of money to keep their looks. Jack wanted to punch his father in the face but didn't. He just wanted to know the answer to one question. He laughs now, sitting across from Mavis, picturing his skinny fourteen-year-old self back then, having the gall to find his dad and ask him why he'd just pulled out and left him and his mother. Jack stood with both feet planted in a man's stance, arms swung to his sides, fingers itching to clench into a fist, waiting for an answer. He was taller than the old man, but thin as a reed in the wind, swaying and waiting, curious to hear what he'd say. The old guy stammered and said something vague about it just not working out. That he and his mother just didn't get along, her being Indian and all that, how he'd been young and she was beautiful and he just got weak for her and married her. It was a mistake, clear and simple. That later he met another woman he had more in common with. "Compatible," was the word that hung in the air between then. Then silence fell and Jack let it. The question was still there. He let his father sweat. He was an old guy, had been tall but was bent as if he'd been sitting at a desk too long and had a bad back. He was red in the face; a clammy sweat gathered on the old brow and began to drip down, even in the chill of the fog that hung in the air out in that California seacoast city. He pulled out a clean folded handkerchief and mopped his face and then tried to lay a hand on his son's shoulder, clap him like a business deal, a conspiracy of confidence, a me-and-you-and-them style.

Jack stepped back, waited, and in a tone that even surprised himself, said, "That's about her. Why'd you leave me." Again the businessman's grin of impatience, eager to get the deal over with. "That's the way it was. That's the way it is. That's...." and he threw out his hands and shrugged. I figured she'd take you back to the reservation, Son, and you'd be raised an Indian, you know. You had her dark hair at birth, a lot of it, just like a papoose." He chuckled at little like a red-necked bigot. A real chump. Then, he reached into the breast pocket of his lapel and brought out a checkbook, a flat leather thing, a rich man's wallet. Jack saw the gold ring on his father's hand, a thick one. "Now, how much do you want, Son? How much do you think you need? I can't make it up to you, you know that. But you've got a pair of balls to come here, you know that don't you? How about a couple of thousand to get you started somewhere, you know there's that equal opportunity thing now. People's got to hire you. Can't discriminate. You've got your rights."

Jack shook his shaggy head, working his jaw bone, and said, "I can't let you do that. I just came to take a look at you to satisfy myself." He could see the blur of a woman behind the curtains on the picture window. He could never forget her posture. She was worried, looking, trying to eavesdrop. And then he walked away. "I never saw the guy again. He's got grown sons of his own who work for the company. He's a grandfather. Everybody loves the guy in that town. His name is on billboards. I don't hold any grudges. He's just a weak son of a bitch, that's all. And I'm okay. I wasn't going to let him pay me off to salve his conscience. And it doesn't do any good to eat my heart out over what I didn't get, what I didn't have growing up. I did alright on my own. If I'd stayed around, the only difference, is I'd be all dressed up in a suit sitting at a desk selling real estate. The thought of that scares me. I feel trapped just at the idea of it. I'd probably own a lot of stuff, have spent a lot of money, forty years accumulating things, spending, buying. Being a consumer. This way I've gotten out of all that. Haven't left a trail of material waste in my wake. I've got just me and my views on things." Jack came to, so to speak, and noticed Mavis again, so caught up in memory. Mavis had watched how the words came out and loved his mouth, the way it moved, his wide sensual outdoor mouth, smooth and rosied by the sun; and the male resonance of his voice. She heard no bitterness there, and saw no resentment in the ready smile that turned up in the corners of his mouth as quick as a kid's. He was Tom Sawyer and Huckleberry Finn, Lil' Abner in one. He was not a character from of a Dickens' tale, though the sadness could be there. He looked at Mavis, smiled for the indulgence of talking so long, showing perfect white boyish teeth.

Mavis supressed a desire to go to him and hug him and make it all up to him, the pain of his childhood. She knew Jack would ward off any pity. He was telling his story as a matter of fact and not for sympathy. She would not insult him by petting him as if he really were a poor stray dog. He had survived quite well and was, by all appearances, well-adjusted; while she, herself, who had gotten everything given to her was not even happy. She had been frustrated for too many years so that it filtered everything she did. By all appearances she should be happy. She had everything. What was it Jack had inside him that gave him his ability to get more out of life than she could so that he could easily swing into her life and sit there more comfortable than she. Mavis sighed. Jack knitted his brows, looking at her response to his story, afraid that it may have upset her. Perhaps she wanted to comfort him now and be the mother of the fourteen-year-old on the road. She was always ready to feed him, that was obvious. Did he still give the impression of being that hungry boy. He waited for her to comment and she never did, just looked down into her lap and sat there. He knew she was afraid to say anything lest it sound as if she were patronizing him. He knew women with homes looked upon him and wanted to shelter him.

chapter six

When Jack was through, Mavis began telling her storyline, barebones and brief, just to match age for age, decade for decade: born in this beach town, grew up here, married briefly after college. UCLA., at first. Met Bill there. He was a business major. She'd studied graphic design, even back then when computers were just coming out for the public; and now made a living at it. No children. Couldn't get pregnant, in fact. She'd tried to have children during her marriage to Bill. It wasn't him. Yes, she still wanted a child, even at forty-three. There was the biologies, that craving to tend and love a small helpless dependent being of her own creation. At this point, she stared at the air and was very still, contemplating such a miracle. Jack said nothing. Just waited, eyes resting on her, interested in the individual words she chose, the content of her story, seeing her expression and hearing the intonation, seeming to learn something he'd missed out on that was vital to his own sense of order in the universe. He listened to Mavis' story, watching her, as if at the movies, studying the way she moved her hands when she spoke, the knitting or raising of her eyebrows, the working of the corners of her mouth, curious about what happened next and next and next up to the present moment; half expecting she'd say, "And then I met this wonderful guy under the pier....YOU!" He saw her one-time live-in relationship with her husband after her beach life childhood, a nice house, two parents who never divorced and moved to Florida to retire. They'd given up waiting for a grandchild. She was their only child. Her father was a civil engineer. He'd designed bridges; her grandfather had helped build the Golden Gate Bridge, in fact, way back. That was her claim to fame, and she gave one simple laugh here to illustrate how silly the family pride was. Her mother was just a housewife, although she'd studied fashion design as an art student and then changed it to architecture, held a B.A., but never used it.

"My mother came over from England and met my father in college. She never went back, married, and lost touch with her side of the family. She was an only child who was adopted as a baby by a couple who couldn't have children. My mother was a product of college campus sex. She was an accident. The student put her up for adoption in London. In those days there was no abortion and an unwed mother was a disgrace. Her parents never came over from England after my mother moved to the United States. She had married an American student studying civil engineering. They'd walk on the London Bridge and he'd tell her all about how it was constructed," she laughed. "They were very British and, I think, felt betrayed that she'd marry a lowly American." She laughed again.

Her voice had become too breezy as if her life was a ball. Mavis switched voices and went on after that long aside in a simple documentarian tone, leaving the jolly lilt out of it. "I had a quiet childhood, typical of the local life style; going to the beach and park for picnics, being the darling of parents who loved me." Mavis said this as if it had bound her to be good and do the right thing, looking up at Jack to see if he was proud of the freedom he'd had by contrast. She'd been given every lesson a child is given in hopes something would take: tennis, swimming, sailing, horsemanship, arts and crafts, most stringed musical instruments. The art took. She was sent off to school with all the trimmings, dorm, wardrobe, even sorority. But, she'd never been a cheerleader type, thank goodness. Too serious for that. She went to Berkeley. Just when all hell broke loose: the feminists were raging, Civil Rights movement was rampant, and the Hippies, drug, sex, and rock and roll anti-establishmentarianism in the throes of bringing down the big men on top and rejuggling the whole traditional pyramid of power. She laughs again at her own notions and the pronunciation of that long word that was so popular back then.

"I was never a featherhead or a rebel." She stops and laughs apologetically, shrugging at her privileged upbringing and the choices she had. "I was studious. Serious. I was quiet, not too social. I liked to read a lot and stay in the dorm when all the girls and guys were gone off somewhere. I liked my solitude," she says, looking up at Jack's rapt attention. "Just like you?" She ventured it as a question to see if he agreed although his was foisted upon him and hers was a choice, but nevertheless, they had that in common, she hoped. Two solitary people finding each other. How could that work out?

They spent the afternoon talking, getting to know the other; and when, at last, they look up, they see that it's late in the day again. Still musing over the companionship that has developed, Mavis consults with Jack on dinner plans, as if they'd been together a long time. She doesn't feel like the hostess with a guest; but as his partner, already. She says, "What do you feel like? I've got lots of food. That's the one thing I like, is a fridge and pantry full." She laughs at herself and adds, "My parents were from the depression generation. Somehow, keeping a stockpile in store in case of unforseen need was bred in.

Jack takes the cue. He shifts in his seat, leans toward Mavis, elbows on his knees, takes her hands in his and says, raising his eyebrows for permission, "I would like to cook for you." Mavis is taken aback, displaced and caught off guard. He says, "I learned a few recipes on the road. Just got to go pick up a few things," and before Mavis could protest or offer more from her own larder so he wouldn't get away from her, he was gone.

She sat there for moments, as if in a stupor, looking at the door; and found herself doubting that he'd be back. A certain possessiveness had come over her which was foreign to her. Her doubt turned to a pensive state where she studied her fingernails and recalled the past twenty-four hours.

Her muscles were sore from making love. Funny how you don't use certain parts of the anatomy except when having sex. Even though she ran, walked, did yoga, sat on the floor in front of the T.V. at night and did exercises and stretches, none of it had reached as deeply into her buttocks or stomach muscles as making love did. The reaching for him with every cell of her body, copulating, clasping, with her whole insides had given her a good workout; and she flexed those muscles now and felt the newly tapped usage of them. The gluteus maximus, the abs. Even her arms and legs where she clung to him and rode and rode and rode him, like in the song by Cat Stevens. She basked in her body, in the aftermath of his abrupt departure. In his absence, she returned to her self. How quickly certain parts are awakened. While she contemplated on the wonders of sexual clutchings and muscle use she wasn't even aware of during the throes of sexual passion, there was a knock on the door. She came out of her reverie and called, knowing it was Jack; her friends never knocked. "Come in," and marvelled that he was back; and it couldn't have been just a moment.

"You haven't moved," he said, with a nonchalant smile, carrying a bag into the kitchen, calling back to her, "It'll be about forty-five minutes... and then he ignored her for fifteen minutes, rattling around behind the counter partition in the kitchen. Her cupboard doors opened and closed, refrigerator sucked open and shut. Mavis got up, padded around her place like an intruder, feeling suddenly awkward, so used to cooking, unused to being cooked for. Bill never cooked. Her father never cooked. She didn't know a man who cooked. She pictured Jack going down to the bird refuge and killing a duck or something, finding a paper sack in a garbage can to put it in and bringing it home. How'd he buy anything from the store? He must have, though. There was no blood and guts or evidence of feathers. Besides, the birds were protected and only in the pitch black of night did the homeless ever kill one and roast it over a fire on the beach at the BBQ pits. She'd heard sad stories of this kind.

Mavis sat at her computer and scanned in a face that resembled an abstraction of Jack. First the mouth, those fabulous lips, then teeth, a smile appeared on her monitor, then eyes, a deep brow, and then the chiseled nose, finely sketched ears, and hair, that tousled wolf's mane, wild and sunstreaked, that he kept running his mighty yet agile fingers through to tame it and look respectable. He had used her comb. She'd saved the few single strong hairs from it just for fun. It was odd to be separate from Jack, he in the kitchen, she at her work station, doodling, unable to concentrate except on his image. She took paint brushes from the menu and began coloring him in, when she felt him touch her shoulder and turned her gently in her office chair on wheels with the swivel seat, kneeled down at her feet, placing a basin of water and a towel on the floor. He said, "I'm going to wash your feet. Just sit there. Close your eyes. I've always wanted to do this." Mavis leaned back, obedient, uncomfortable at first. Her tough California soles? Did he think of them as sand-worn and battered or what? Had he seen some tar on her sole while making love. The beach was covered with it along the tide line and she didn't always get it off. "Close your eyes," he instructed softly again. "Shhh. Let me…"

She rested her head on the chair's head rest, didn't close her eyes entirely, watching him through slits, as Jack took each foot in turn, bathed it in cool water, dried it, massaged it, cradling it in his gentle palms, and then kissed it and then licked it. As he licked her sole, she grew warmer than she had ever been. His tongue was soft and persistent and hot. Why did she assume it would be raspy like a cat's? She felt his breath on her instep. He put each toe in his mouth. He all but slobbered over her feet until she thought he might have a fetish but quelled the conjecture. She would try to let go and be in the moment and not try to figure him out. Maybe he was simply the most sensual man she'd ever known. No man had ever touched her feet. They'd gone right to her crotch as if that's all they knew or cared about, using their penis like a well witcher uses a willow branch. Honing into what would pleasure their nerve endings. As Jack took parts of her feet into his mouth, French kissing them as if they were delicious morsels he loved to roll around on his tongue and savor, she grew so hot her sex flowed and wet the chair. A feeble protest to get a towel and protect her chair came and went, overpowered by sexual abandon. Again he turned Mavis into a wanton lump of flesh, licking her like a lollipop. She was HIS, as he'd whispered that morning. "You're mine," when he knew she was at the point of no return. He built up such desire this way that Mavis grew weak in the knees. Still he didn't touch her between the legs. Through her slits she saw him watching her sex swell and become ready for him, wet, on fire, swollen and pulsating as his hot tongue licked her ankles and then, guided by her groans, kissed inside her calves and up inside her thighs, until her anticipation that he would touch her sex set her own tongue aloll and eyes rolled up, as he retreated down the inside of her legs to her feet. He knew her body, following the arousal, allowing her to build desire and lead him. He stayed behind the surge of passion, and knew was driving her crazy, causing the craving to be touched all the way up so strong she finally cried out, demanding it, and flung her head back, thrusting her breasts out and her pelvis up off the chair and forward into his lips. He was there, kissing her sex as if it were her mouth, his tongue inside licking her everywhere, softly finding her hottest spots and knowing how to tease and be gentle and then forceful. She exploded in his mouth, flowing all over the chair, soaking the expensive absorbent upholstered seat. *Is this why they pad the seats?* was a fleeting notion, just as he offered her his penis, bringing himself up to her mouth. She opened, as if her mouth was a vagina, while he thrust she licked and sucked and held on until she felt hot semen strike the back of her throat, and then he plunged himself between her legs and they groaned together, hotter than she thought she could ever be, abandoned of her senses. Losing herself until he stopped moving, stayed inside, and spoke to her like a rider to a runaway mare, "There, you're mine. I have you. Shhh: Easy, now, easy." She groaned, "Don't stop." He said, "Shhh, hold still, let's make it last." She protested, "No, no, noooool" and grabbed his hips and wiggled her own, moving him and went off again, helplessly gone into orgasm, gasping, shouting, wet, slobbering, drooling, vacant-eyed, mouth agape. "Hahhh!" The great single huff of air as Jack ejaculated. Sound for sound, gutturals answering gutturals, like beasts, the language of love-making. Never having been good at oral sex, Mavis was responding like a porn star. She pictured herself that way in her mind's eye, as she writhed with Jack, as the actress in a film she saw once, performing eroticism.

Suddenly they smelled something burning. "Oh, the dinner," he laughed, pulled out and was off with his member bouncing in the air, wet, glistening, leading him into the kitchen. She smiled out loud, laughter in primitive grunts, weak, bewildered. Where was she. Who was she now? He had taken her over completely again.

She'd read about men like this who can reduce women to sex slaves who knew women's bodies. Sensual men who know how to make love. True lovers. She'd been only with fuckers before, she realized now. Cocksmen. This was all new to her; this total sexuality while "making love." And it took her forty-three years to experience it. With other men, she wondered when they'd be through, impatient. They didn't seem to include her anyway. Used her like a hole in the ground. She'd even thought of other things while they were "doing it." She'd never been this involved before, with every cell of her body focussed on the act, craving it, begging for it. Jack insisted she be present. He listened to her sounds and watched, and felt, and sensed her body respond. She lay limp on the floor where she'd flopped, still swollen and languid as a tropical venus fly trap after satisfying its appetite. Full of whatever a woman fills with that keeps her heavy and in one place after sex. When Jack appeared, this time he held a tray with something steaming in a pot. He placed the tray on the floor and she smelled the ingredients. Chicken soup! There were two bowls, two glasses of wine, a baguette of grained sourdough. She smiled. Yes! She needed nourishment for strength. "One of my on-the-road recipes," he said with mirth in his eyes over her inability to rise.

chapter seven

They slept that night like a married couple, familiar and comfortable, her leg flopped over him, he flat on his back with his hands behind his head, arms up, elbows jutting off the pillow, completely at home, relaxed. In the wee hours she awoke and saw the half moon travelling across the sky, got up and parted the curtains so moonlight would illuminate his face. It seemed she had known him forever, that a place in her had always made a place for him and now he had come home to live there. She studied his strong nose and sharp jaw and saw his ancestors in tribal dress, along with the Swedes and English. She felt their attraction, male to female, so strong that they intermarried. Her eyes toyed with the way his eyelashes lay against those cheekbones and the nostrils of a stallion, always flared, inhaled and exhaled in silence while his lips, slightly parted showed a hint of alabaster teeth. She listened to his breathing slow and deep and longed to go there and inhale his breath and make it hers. She wanted to be him, to crawl up under his flesh and be the strong, unscathed male he was, able to shed threats without scars, to hide her vulnerable female self inside his strong ribcage where she would be safe, and know him from the inside and how it was being him. A vein stood out on the coarse flesh of his neck, matching the one she had seen on the long strong stem of his penis. Blood to brain and body, each well supplied by a single engorged vein. She watched the hair jutting from every pore rise and fall in the rhythm of deep sleep, that other world he was in while she bathed him with loving eyes. She smiled, remembering her friend say, "A large part of me missed him," about a boyfriend she'd had once. Sue had a large behind. "Yes," she thinks, now, "A large part of me craves him." She thought of her heart, since her bodyl-was slight and no part was very large. Sleep was a waste, she thought, while he's with me. Every moment I sleep, I miss seeing him, taking him in. In the hour of the wolf, as that Swedish film maker used to call it, Mavis felt certain that after this kind of heat, their chemistry, the connection their bodies felt, they would be together as a couple. It would be a violation of the law of nature for them to part, for him to be able to walk away and not look back, not after the way he knew how to touch her and send her into spasms of eroticism; not after guiding her and teaching her to go there, to open up, to not hold back, to give in to sex, to not try to control it but to let it control her, let him control her, to lose control and by letting go gaining more than she could imagine.

Mavis fell asleep, claiming Jack with her thigh over his groin, wondering if a man like Jack could be a kept man and domesticated. Is he like those wild mustangs they round up feeling trapped when they run into the confines of the fence, so used to no boundaries. Will a house look like a cage to him. Is he only a male animal, a sleek feline mating, making contact with a female, and then wandering off to be alone. Can he live inside a home and not just in the cab of a truck heading out? Or on foot with his thumb out? She felt hopeless. They hadn't talked about the big "C" word, commitment. It was too soon. And he hadn't given any hints of wanting to stay around and have her be his woman. He simply had gone along with the days of love-making as if biding his time. She had watched his face in the throes of sex and saw no sign of abandonment, but a steady concentration, the skill of taking a woman and turning her into a frothing and foaming at the mouth sexual creature, of taking her over and having her, the way a male animal finally gets the female to submit after all the screeching and fanging and clawing. Why did she always think of him as a cat. His stealth. Was that the Indian in him. His incredible masculinity and awareness of everything all around him and how he was affecting it. Why didn't he say anything to assuage her fear that he might leave. He certainly felt it by her own generosity to him, that he was now included in her life. Her friend, Sue, told her of using the word "we" once and the then boyfriend at the time said, "We are NOT a *we*." Mavis drifted into sleep feeling foolish…in bed with a man who would most certainly not be contained by her art deco walls, would soon escape when she least expected it. A man she knew only by her emotions and not by any reasoning whatsoever.

They awoke, stretched, letting their eyes search for and find the other, yawned, smiled, and lay there happy in that moment. It was meant to be; Mavis felt deeply again all through her. It felt right. Her beautiful surroundings embraced them, cradling them with light playing into the room, highlighting walls to look transluscent and then retreating to leave them matte and dark; while her artwork teased them and played with their mood. Jack seemed satisfied. She watched him like a hawk and tried not to. She felt as in love with him as she had been at twelve with that boy next door two years younger than herself, but tall for his age. The same qualities in him as Jack had, a healthy innocence and shrewd knowing in one. She remembers, his name was Travis. In fact, he looked like Jack. It was coming back to her. No wonder there was a deeper recongition of Jack than vision. She had known him emotionally, erotically in her puberty in that way a girl gets a crush. Though, she and Travis never touched, he had set Mavis into fantasies that had just now come true with Jack. She didn't know what sensual abandon meant back then, or sensual heat, but she remembers being lazy and open and lying on the bed feeling funny thinking of Travis back then. She learned later that that feeling was what Sue called "horny." "Ha, you were horny, that's all, and didn't even know what it was. Ha!"

In the aftermath of sleep, they murmured to each other like any paired beasts, sounds of familiarity. Mavis ventured into Jack's intentions cautiously, without words, watching for signs. It was out of character for her to beat around the bush and say things indirectly; but she feared his answers to direct questions. She couldn't just say, "Do you plan to move in now, marry me, and we will live happily ever after?" Or, "Will you live with me for the rest of your life and we can stay in this state of bliss forever?" Or, "I don't know how you feel, but

I'm in ecstasy and want to be with you always." Or, "How do you feel about us?" It would give Jack the break he needed to answer straight, be frank, and probably break her heart. He wouldn't hem and haw. He hadn't done any mealy mouth talk yet. He was honest enough not to be evasive if she asked directly. So, she didn't dare ask him point blank what he felt or intended to do regarding her.

They passed a month this way, loving, working, eating together, watching the moon in its stages across the night sky. The moon was very much a part of their lives, peeking in the big glass windows, throwing gold and silver against the walls, the bed, their faces as they writhed in love or slept. The moon illuminated their loving as long as it could and then darkness fell and Mavis worried. Jack talked about going back to driving truck briefly when he saw her hard at work, sitting hours in front of her computer printing out reams of completed jobs. She listened to his plans to go back to work and be steady at it, make a living again. Get structured. What a word for Jack to use. She toyed with it all day, thinking it over and over and what it could mean.

"Structured." In regard to what? Was he hinting for her to open the topic of his drifting and offer something? She vowed not to be the first one to put it in words. Her behavior spoke loud and clear. If he couldn't read something in that, well, then...

She could never finish. What would she say, "Then, too bad, you lose." There was only their nebulous touchings and strenuous strainings in sinew to go by. Mavis, usually blunt to the point of tactlessness, remained mute on the subject of asking Jack to stay in her life and risk rejection. This tension kept them together like teeter-totters. Once spoken, the balance would be off and she might find herself picking herself up. With nothing but time on his hands, Jack made himself useful. He tended her house plants, repotting the tiny palm tree and fertilizing the mango seed he'd also potted. Outdoors he groomed the plants with loving care, wearing her loosest t-shirts and shorts, walking around with his member half erect, with it bobbing as he moved about bare-footed and half apologetic. He laundered his worn jeans and t-shirt along with her clothes, folding them from the dryer better than she did. He cooked. He was a marvelous cook, making a pasta sauce that set her tongue a-drooling. His stews and soups and roasted meats set her nose to twitching in anticipation. He brought home meats with sexy names like tenderloin, tongue, heart, rump, rib, and made her laugh like a child over the fun of it. She was not even a meat eater until Jack showed her how you put it on a spit and let the fat drip off. He used the BBQ or the roasting spit of her oven. She taught him how to make tofu taste good. He was a quick learner and threw himself into braising tofu in sauces of his own concoction. Every time Jack disappeared to go on runs to the grocery store, Mavis' heart would wilt a little, until she heard his footstep on the path; then her heart would fill and sing, "He didn't leave me, he didn't leave me." It was a mystery where Jack got money to buy food. He refused to take money from Mavis. Did he do the odd job to get enough to buy groceries or what? He never explained and she never asked. Had he accepted money from his father after all. Did he have a savings account and an invisible ATM card. Did he get disability from the Seabees or a truck injury. Her head was awhirl with curiosity.

It was comforting to hear a man puttering around her once still and quiet home, where, if there was a sound, she was the only one to make it. Jack was neat and tidy and quick and skilled in housekeeping. Maybe the Seabees taught him, she mused. Or, his mother. Or the road. How was a drifter so good at organizing the tasks of homemaking. It remained a mystery to Mavis. He made a very good wife while she labored at her desk. Just what I've needed, she thought. She'd look up now and then as he passed by, giggling at his nearly nude hulk in her baggiest cottons, giddy as a girl. The comparisons to Bill had stopped. There was no comparison, she figured. She had outgrown using Bill as a reference point for a male now that she had been with Jack for three quarters of a moon. They had begun to clock their time together by the moon, instigated by her teasing him with having a sixth sense about most things attributing it to his Indian blood. He just smiled and played along, telling her the time of day by the sun and the night by the moon, teasing her back.

In those beautiful long days with Jack in the house, Mavis wore raw spots on her knees, kneeling to nuzzle Jack's heroic musk scent. She'd waylay him on the way through the room, pull down his pants and nuzzle into his aromatic pubic hair while he stood helpless, compliant, always a gentleman. One afternoon, when she was thus prostrating herself willingly, out of her need to inhale him, he gently took her head and had her stand facing him. With steady eyes he told he wanted her to come with him. He wouldn't tell her where. It was something he wanted her to see. The way he said, "Come with me. I want to show you something," enthralled her. She followed him out the door and down through the neighborhood on foot Indian guide style. She, the white and trusting the greater intelligence out here in the wood. "Three paces behind," began an unspoken chant, as she tried to keep up with his intense stride. He stopped and turned to wait for her where the street turned and he intended to go off the walkway into the underbrush. He held back a branch and motioned for her to enter; and she did. This is very clever, she thought, somber and obedient. He commands and I respond without a word. She finally resorted to being female, squealing when a manzanita bush reached out and tore at her legs. "Jack? What is this? Where are you taking me." She thought of serial killers who live awhile with their victims. The hair on her scalp stood out. She thought, "Scalp," yet she still followed Jack, as he crept now, bent without a sound, holding brush back so she wouldn't get slapped in the face with it, as she also crouched and entered into this thicket with him. At last, Jack stood full height, and held the last branch, so Mavis could also enter into the clearing. He fastened his eyes on Mavis' face as she stood staring at what was before her. There was a campsite with firepit and big stones to sit on, in the middle and all around were sapling palms of varying sizes growing in rows. It looked like a nursery. The earth had been tilled and made ready for yet more little trees. Mavis looked up at Jack for an explanation. He said, "This is where I live." She began to laugh.

"Are these all the little palms you've saved from the tide, Jack?" She grinned into his face but was cut short by his sober expression.

"Yes," was his answer, his face closed shut like a door to a guest who dared to trivialize what was a point of pride to him. Mavis stared at the grove of tiny palm with their fibrous tough spears of frond reaching up for their place in the world, encircling the firepit like little marching soldiers. How little she knew Jack. Is this where he goes when he leaves me? This saving little plants and nurturing, not only palm, but others. She sees plants everywhere now that her eyes have adjusted to the reality of the place. Jack takes her on a walking tour, pointing-out plants that stores had thrown out in dumpsters, others people had dumped into garbage cans for daring to wither in the pot and shame them. Jack, a rescuer of discarded and endangered plant life. A man who saves poor helpless things and gives them a chance in this rich soil he's cultivated among the native plant life. His secret garden. Mavis' hair rises on her scalp again and she gets goose bumps and her throat tightens. This Jack she didn't even know and now he trusts me, enough to reveal him, to bring me here, to let me see his insides. Who he really is. What matters to him. What he believes in. This is his art. His work. And all unsung, unseen. She is shamed, somehow, feeling small in the company of a good man. She didn't know. In all the throes of sex, she didn't know about his caring like this. The time he's spent. The way he can't not do it. His devotion. This is his strength, she thinks. This is how he saves himself. These are his children, his love. She bends to see a recovering primrose, touches a delicate fuchsia hidden in the shade of large palm, strokes the wild efforts of a hibiscus trying to hang onto life, and kneels humbly on the ground with her head bowed. Jack squats beside her and points to the way a creeping vine has found its way to a slant of sunshine.

chapter eight

And then the full moon appeared again. In Indian language they'd known each other one moon! She was dreaming of a logo about their love and putting it on stationery, making greeting cards, posters, t-shirts, on all kinds of things. She was inspired in the dream and envisioned symbols of her love for Jack everywhere. It was on this night, the night of the full moon that Mavis awoke to find Jack gone from her bed. The emptiness had awakened her. Her thigh rested on the coolness of the sheet not against his body heat. Her body knew first; and then she rose up on one elbow and saw him through the glass doors outside on the deck off the bedroom. His silouhette stood stark against the moonlight, facing out away from her in a wirey tension. It was the way he was standing, this new posture, that unnervered her. He leaned at an angle ever so slightly as if sniffing the air with the concentrated stillness of a trapped animal. Mavis sat upright and studied Jack from the back, the full moon on the water and in his face. She could only imagine the look he must have of longing to go, to travel, to be on the road, the way he held his head alert for a cue, waiting to catch the scent of direction. Or, what? Something was tugging at him and he seemed to be pulling back. A tug of war in the way he braced himself. She began to breathe again after the initial shock of discovering him out there away from her, away from the bed they had shared for what seemed forever in its rightness, from seeing him at the railing of her property with such a stance of urgency. She took a deep breath and watched, helpless to hold him. She'd seen his many postures for many days and thought she knew his body language, but not this one. Weary, Mavis went back to sleep without interrupting

Jack's mood. She drifted off, giving up and giving in to fate. *What will be will be,* she heard Doris Day screeching the song at the top of her lungs. How could she trap a wild animal and force him to stay in a cage and try to domesticate him. All that she loved about Jack was there in his wild and free and independent stature. It was his strength. He knew how to go, not to stay. He'd never learned to stay and bow down; and he didn't know how to stay and hold his head up and fit into the daily routine. Mavis hoped it was only her imagination and fear of his leaving that made her see Jack this way, as longing to move on. She slept uneasy and when she awoke at daybreak he was gone, leaving no trace that he had ever existed except for a t-shirt. It was one of her over-sized t-shirts full of his scent. She, now became an Indian scout, holding the shirt to her nose, inhaling his body odor, that clean male sweat that had no trace of deodorant. His sweat was one not of fear from adrenalin, but of heat from movement. He was a hot body not a scared one. He sweat making love to her. He sweat over the stove making dinner for her. He sweat in the sun on the deck, reading from her library. It was the sweat of a man moving about, being active, not from running from a predator. It was the same for Mavis. The only time she had offensive sweat was during her divorce. She used to tell people this. It was the only time she had to wear deodorant. She knew the difference between fearful sweat that lets off an offensive odor to scare away enemies and the clean sweat from daily living. Mavis pulled Jack's t-shirt on, swearing to keep it forever and wear it every day, believing it would bring him back. She'd done that once for a lost dog and it worked. He followed his nose back to his own scent. Mavis thought how much she was acting like an animal. Where had the pre-Jack Mavis gone to? Scent to lure, is it?

Once upright, out of bed and padding around her home, alone for the first time in a month, Mavis trudged leadened and lonely. Her first impulse was to get in her car and go looking for him, but quelled it with a broken-spined hautiness, trying to hold her head up with pride and in the same instance, keeled forward as if punched in the stomach. She found it hard to breathe. Pins and needles of pain shot through her body and kept her fingers and toes tingling as if withdrawing from a drug. There must be some mistake, she thought, but remembered his silouhette, as if howling, long and silent, at the moon; communicating with the great out there, while she lay, too small and too female to compete with his need for traveling on. She'd given her all and if that didn't hold him, what could? His autonomy, in the only way he knew how to maintain it, apparently meant more to him than she did. Or was it the way she responded to his palm garden. Was he wounded by her laughter. Was he so vulnerable? Did showing her his secret place mean more to him than she knew? And who would tend his dear plants if he'd moved on out of town. Did he stay only for the dry season and know they'd survive during the wet season without him? Mavis knew she would frequent Jack's palm garden looking for him, even against her will. The Mavis Jack had created would go in search of her mate with the will of a warrior. Yet, the Mavis she had been before Jack kept her home behind her computer, trying to carry on, anguishing.

Still her ears were alert for any sound of his coming back, a creak at the door, footfalls on the gravel path, a cough, clearing of the throat, a bark of a dog announcing someone passing, a scuff of chair on the deck. She pictured him there, flashed memories of him all over her place, sitting, standing, lying, smiling, sleeping, making sounds behind closed doors, rattling around in the kitchen, yard, and then kept imagining him returning, walking in after first knocking softly, the big wide white smile, the mirth in his eyes, the concern that she had been hurt by his absence, his perception of her feelings, his intuitive face, knowing without having to ask and be told. He never asked how she was feeling. He always knew. He must have known the night he left that she had risen up and saw what she saw in him. He would have read the bed clothes and how she tossed and turned as he tiptoed away from her and her walls and away to his freedom. "Enslaved to his freedom, he is," Mavis said aloud. "He is a slave to his freedom. There is no such thing as freedom if you are driven to go get it and have it all the time." She became obstinate, setting her lips in a thin straight line.

In waiting for Jack's return, Mavis grew disheartened hour by hour; and when twenty-four hours passed, and then day by day, with the full moon waning and a month went by without a word, she could hardly move through a day, did not dress, slept hard and awakened with wet eyes. When the moon waxed full again, Mavis sat on her deck in the same chair he had made love to her in; well, where hadn't they made love; every place, including the tiled sink board and wherever they found themselves, perching, standing, lying, sitting, leaning. They were like a couple of adolescents discovering the wonders of their bodies. Her home had been initiated by love, at last. And now, only the stains on the upholstery she refused to clean to remove his scent, were left as any evidence that Jack had been there. And that baby palm growing vigorously in its pot with the good mulch; and, of course that blasted mango seed. Amazing that Jack got that to grow. He was good at planting seeds which struck her as odd for a nomad. Must be the Swedish pioneer blood of farmers coming through to override the wandering tribal side. No one gets a mango seed to grow here; they grow in Mexico or Hawaii, yet, the tree had sprouted into a sapling with a stalk that looked like his penis. Mavis got up, heavy on her runner's feet, tired from mourning her loss, and leaned in the same way he had against the railing of her deck, facing the vast sea, trying to see what he saw, feel what he felt that night. She play-acted Jack, leaning on the railing at the same angle, trying to feel what he must have been feeling, trapped by the limited space of her deck; knowing it was against his nature to have stayed from moon to moon.

She saw herself, the fool, lying without bone or sinew, completely under his spell during that time span. Doubts crept in. Did she misread his actions, translate all those orgasms and mumurings as love and constancy? Did she interpret his presence for thirty days as domestication and believe that in one fell swoop he'd become a house boy, her man, a man who would stay with a woman forever after? In view of his disappearance, Mavis shamed herself this way and a deep red-faced embarrassment came on strong. She'd held nothing back. She'd never given herself without reserve before. And, he'd egged her on with those guiding words, like rider to horse the way she used to talk to calm her horse in competition as a girl. He'd steered her into territory she'd never been, urged to go and go and go, and taught her that she could go there and jump the highest obstacles and do it. She could go where he took her, giving up resistance, caution, trusting him, leaving common sense behind, leaping and soaring into sensuality, opening her body like never before. And now, as far as she soared, she fell and fell and fell, downward, spiraling to the bottom, hitting hard. She felt old and tired and drained of life's force. No blood coursed through her veins now. She was dead, kept the curtains closed, moped, sat at her work station and stared at the air, got behind in deadlines, let go of all the daily things, grooming, eating, working; fighting feelings of being stupid and dumb. She hid all the print-outs, photos and sketches she'd done of Jack, pulling them off the wall with a vengeance. With Bill she had always retained a kernel of herself, never abandoned her idenity, had sex without losing control. She'd never gotten lost like she did with Jack, melding, molding, conforming, bonding with another human being, woman or man, in this way. The memory of his power over her lurked like evil in hindsight. Whatever had possessed her to give herself up to him. Why was she so helpless in his arms. Ah, his arms came back to her in all their glory. The way he knelt on knees and elbows over her, taking her. She tried to put it out of mind, vacillating between a deep shame to have been so deceived and an anger toward his deceit, and the memory of the thrill of passion. Questions were scarce as they came and went, barely surfacing to consciousness. Why did he act so perfect, say the right thing, seem sincere? Were these the proverbial Casanova qualities and she a sitting duck? Was she so transparent and he a con artist? So he had a soft heart for plants. So what! Mavis took to watching T.V. at night to distract herself from the pain. The news came and went and movies and sitcoms came and went. One night there was a lot of fuss being made over some truck that'd made a mess of things on some east coast turnpike somewhere. That had taken her attention, reminding her of Jack and his truckers before she stopped herself and put him out of her mind for the hundreth time. That was what Sue said she was told to do by her therapist. You just make yourself stop thinking of him when he comes into your thoughts and that's that. Pretty soon you will be over him. Sue also took the bull by the horns and dragged her out to a wild place called the Palomino Club, trying to shock Mavis out of grieving over Jack. There were men on stage stripping and an audience of women cheering. Next, Sue took her to the local bowling alley Country Western dance night where cowboys and cowgirls shuffled around in boots to a song that sent tears streaming down Mavis' cheeks called *These Four Walls*, or something like that. She felt trapped in her own house now. The walls seemed to have moved in on her. It was the only reason she let Sue get her out of there; but to no avail. Once home again, the walls stood staring at her.

Mavis went to her deck every morning to tend and water the palm and mango plants with their brand new tender leaves quivering in the sunshine. She cursed and praised them in the same breath. Jack seemed to be leering at her with every new shoot of life they sent up to stand and take their rightful place in the sun. He'd saved the tiny palm tree in its infancy from the ravages of rough tides and ocean storms just to cause such torrents inside her breast in his wake. The mango was his statement of sensuality to her. The memory of his mouth, the fruit so like her own anatomy. The hairy seed in the soil actually breaking open and sending down a thread of root, and sending up an erect thick stalk so like his sexuality. She, left with the memory of him in them. Both had broken through the rich soil. Mavis thought they looked like Jack. Both tall and shiny, clean and healthy, unscathed by the soil they'd shed emerging immaculate. Almost smiling in their joy of making it against all odds, moving in the gentle ocean breeze that always bathed her "terrace." That was his word for the deck.

In her sorrow, Mavis stopped bleeding. Or, she believed it was from emotional devastation; and then discovered that Jack had also planted his seed in her, deep and strong, soon to break out into the stark sunlight and live in her arms and at her breast. She was pregnant. She told the doctor that it couldn't be. "I'll be forty-four when the baby comes; and besides, I've never been able to get pregnant. I tried for years when I was married." All her arguments fell on deaf ears and on the constant smile on her doctor's face, while shaking his head, shrugging his shoulders. In eight months, Mavis thought, I will give birth to Jack's child. A smile grew on her face and she couldn't pinch it off. The doctor saw this and patted her on the shoulder, ushering her out of his office. It was true, he nodded in agreement and confirmation; and he saw that Mavis delighted in the prospect. All the way home, in her little car, Mavis marvelled and rejoiced. Jack had not gotten away after all. Ha! He had planted his seed; and she would have a part of him forever. She could have jumped in the air like the cheerleader she'd never been and shouted to the sky, "Yea, yea, yea!" She didn't need pom poms. She was cheering inside. For the baby's sake, she would remember only the good things about Jack. That evening Mavis dug out all the drawings and photos and tacked them back on the wall around her work station. She would, in time, put the ultrasound photos of little Jack next to them. There was her favorite printout of Jack, wide white smile, mirthful eyes, the kindness of caring for lost plants there in the twinkle, and the flairing nostrils, sculpted jawline and perfect male ears. Ah, yes. Jack was more than someone who walked out on her. He was the father of her unborn baby, and the one who showed her the way to real love and wholesome womanliness. She would bring forth the life he had planted and honor it with all the love she had learned from his tender strength.

chapter nine

So, Mavis is pregnant after all the doctors said it couldn't be done without fertility treatment. Leave it to Jack. She smiles over his powers. It was him. She knew that. The feelings he'd cultivated in her for him couldn't help but produce life. She was fertile soil, same as in the palm garden. He'd taken down all her barriers, left her body a garden of Eden, ripe and ready for his seed. He had that way about him. As she reflects on this mysterious quality in Jack, the way he made her female in his arms, under his tutelage. She warms to the memory of the way he had handled her body, turning her up to him with his great hand at the small of her back. She remembered how he lifted her with one hand to position her. His strength, her small body, his naturalness in bringing her to him. She never felt awkward crawling to him or having him over her or under her or beside her. There never were too many arms and legs in bed with them that got in the way. He never tore her long hair out from the roots by accidentally leaning on it with his elbows or hurt her breasts with a clumsy jab. He was as aware of her soft places and bony places as his own, and never too rough or not strong enough. She'd seen horses mating. The stallion was never at a loss on how to go about it. He mounted, magnificent, holding the mare by the mane. He knew what to do, never missed finding IT, never made a mistake. Never wondered, is it in? Never had to be instructed by any other male. In this way Jack got Mavis confused and obedient to his commands the way she used to turn an obstinate horse in circles before it took directions. He made her hormone-rich! Now, for the baby's sake, Mavis vowed to wallow in the memory of how good it was with Jack. There was nothing but good until he left, in fact. His leaving was the only bad. She ran through the nights they had together and settled on the one that was The

One. She had the feeling that night that, if it were possible at all, he had impregnated her. That night she had received his seed wholeheartedly. There was something about it that stood out above the others. He'd gone out again and come home with a duck. A dead duck under cellophane, all picked and ready to roast. He'd put it on the spit and while it turned and sizzled and toasted and was finally ready, they'd sat around naked on the couch and talked, laughed and simply loved being together with the familiarity of their bodies in their mouths as taste; his smell, hers, their skin immersed, so they moved as extensions of each other. Then, Jack got up, strode across to the kitchen nook while she delighted in his small, high, male hindquarters, removed the duck from the spit, cursed a little when he burnt his fingers, stuck them in his mouth to cool them and smacked his lips, tasting the hot meat. Mavis watched him like the best show on T.V. that evening. She smelled the roasted duck from where she sat, anticipated the taste, having gone from being vegetarian before Jack to a carnivore with Jack. From bovine to feline! She saw her life in two pieces: before Jack and after Jack. She had never eaten so much meat since he'd come into her life. On the road, the homeless drifters always manage to find some meat to cook, either wild or from the store, and cook it over a campfire under a bridge or out of sight somewhere. Jack was used to meat as a staple. A wandering man needs his energy and vegetable matter didn't serve him well. She remembered the fire pit in the midst of the palm grove, blackened with the soot of many nights, while Mavis, oblivious of Jack's existence, turned up the thermostat back then. And all the while Jack sat illuminated in fire warming himself as if it were two hundred years earlier, as if half a mile away there was not a woman whose heart was waiting for the likes of him so she could love. While he was with Mavis', Jack brought home the meat, she provided the grains and vegetables, big salads, steamed broccoli that he chuckled over while he ate it, and they got along fine this way with Jack an equal contributor. Where he got the meat, with what resources, she never asked. He walked out the door, and like a hunter, came in with meat in a brown paper sack. She let it be. He cooked meats with sexual names: breast, thigh, tenderloins, leg of lamb, butt, shank, tongue, fillets, and whole fish with the eyes staring, and now duck. She thought, It rhymes with fuck, but knew he didn't use four letter words. He cooked everything but bison, venison, ostrich, or rabbit. She hoped he'd never bring a rabbit home to eat and he never did.

That certain night, the one when she was sure she conceived (what a word in her mindless state), Jack made a salad from her garden, while the duck cooled enough to eat, brought the big salad bowl over in one hand, the duck on a platter in the other, stark naked, his genitals dangling between them, set the plates on the coffee table, and without silverware or napkins, tore the duck in half, neck to tail, handed her a half and sat eating his like a savage, licking his fingers clean, cracking the bones with his molars and sucking out the marrow and finally laying the skeleton on the platter and licking his lips and wiping his mouth with the back of his hand. She again saw that actor doing that in a movie when he played an Indian. She copied him, learning how not to use utensils, getting grease around her mouth, eating off her lipstick, pulling the skin off with her teeth and eating it separately then going after the meat and last, chewing on the bones and crunching down gristle. When she had gnawed her half duck down to a few well-sucked bones, she wiped her face with the back of her hand and then licked her fingers clean. They each ate choice pieces of purple onion, sun ripened tomatoes, and thick-cut lettuce and cucumber from the bowl with their fingers until it was gone, finding a tiny snail in the bowl and taking it outdoors, laughing; then sat back and looked at each other and smiled. She, had been the one to initiate sex that night and for the first time. It was right after this eating orgy. She leaned back, opened her legs and propped her foot up on the coffee table, turned and showed herself, sat facing him with a naughty grin, a proud student, looking at his lap where she could see he was aroused. The alarm on his face was boyish. Yes, he would come and get her. He knew she liked to be "chased through the bushes," as he put it once. "Pursued," was her word. She giggled, slipped to the floor and flaunted her sex. "Take me, take me." Her voice» was deep and hoarse. He slid off the couch and, on elbows and knees, fit himself into her, whispering in her ear, "Oh, you wanton woman, you. Yes, yes." Their muted pleasure sounds answered one another while he moved and she moved and they communicated with love noises beneath language as if one large beast to itself. It was a quiet session of sheer intimacy. The wild bucking and galloping wasn't there that night. Still oily with duck grease they moved gently and made it last and last and Jack caressed her face with nibblings and love bites, dragging his lips over her lips, cheeks, ears, neck. The climax was long and strong and electric. She knew that was the night they made the baby. A love child. One of passion. She was relaxed and used to Jack and to sex and to being naked and to letting him know that she wanted it "IN." Wanted him in. "Put it in. Put it in." Her expression had at first amused Jack as he complied. "Take me. Put it in. Move." Where had she gotten these words. They were her new vocabulary. She'd never used them before with Bill or anyone.

Mavis comes out of her reverie. That was the night she got pregnant. Now she must prepare for the baby. In preparing for the baby, Mavis simply enjoyed everything about being pregnant, even the morning sickness that lasted all day and night; not that it was fun, but for what it meant. At forty-three, it was something of a miracle in itself. She felt fortunate that Mother Nature had found her sound and able to give birth. She resigned herself to being a single mother if Jack never came back. She wanted no other man. That was the part of the talk she told Sue over the phone that soured in her throat. The father of her baby was an ass if he really could disappear. And had. Sue called him "Jack Ass." Mavis didn't try to defend him, but resented Sue. What did she know? When evenings got bad and the missing came on strong, Mavis stopped watching television and used up her evenings reading. There seemed to be murder or violence of some kind on every channel. She'd never forgotten that exceptionally gory truck wreck that all the channels had a few months back. She had changed channels then trying to escape the repetition of it, and now knew she protected her unborn baby by doing so, and finding a love story on the classic movie channel to lift her spirits. That night, she remembers going to bed feeling sorry, sad, and apprehensive and wondered why. Why was she restless and unable to find the usual sense of peace. In the morning she arose with the same uneasiness, did yoga, meditated, and then worked on her projects at the computer. Later that day, she stood looking at all the drawings she had done of Jack as if pulled to them by an invisible, inaudible force.

Mavis tried to settle with the fact that Jack didn't call. Each day when the phone didn't ring, she knew it was him not calling, as that funny country song went, another one she'd heard at the bowling alley with Sue. To prove Jack was gone, Mavis walked to the pier and sat where she and Jack had met, spent a moment of familiarity, as if he still lay leaning on one elbow in the sand. She played voodoo with the spot for awhile and then walked back, got into her car and drove home. In this way she knew for sure that he was not there, in case, somehow, he'd replay that scene, as if it were an act in a play on stage and would be repeated. There was an unreal quality about it, his being there, her getting his seed inside her. Too simple, somehow. She thought about how there was only one first time for anything. Only one first with Jack and that was over. Only once did she happen upon him, just that one time, and have a rare month and now it was behind her. What lay ahead was life, new life, more first times and last times. Each day was a heartbreak and a thrill. Mavis crept into Jack's nursery in the bush to have a look, too. Of course there was no sign of Jack, yet the plants were doing just fine. She knew how they felt. Sure, it would be nice to have him back, but not essential. She was doing just fine, too.

Mavis slept with Jack's t-shirt until his smell turned into her smell or blended into a third smell, the combination of the two of them. She could no longer distinguish between hers and his; and one day, in a fit of pique, she threw the t-shirt into the washer. Enough sentimentality. "I have a baby coming. I will be a mother. No more silliness over some man who chose to run out on his baby the way his own father did; even if he didn't know I was pregnant, he ran, nevertheless, as if in his bloodline it had become an instinct written in the genes."

Mavis rid herself of his wood, leather, horse smell; whatever it was. Her olfactory lobes stored the memory and would know his scent, but she, herself would determine to forget. There were no commercial smells that reminded her of Jack. He never used any on his body. He was simply clean because he lived clean, loved and kissed clean. No nicotine, no rotten teeth at the back, no dandruff, no alcohol, no coffee drinker's burnt out stomach lining, not even the smell of a meat eater. He ate sparse and modest, had a single cup of coffee in the morning, never indulged, gorged or hogged the last bite of anything, except her! Never belched or passed gas in her presence. He was never crude. She had to stop thinking about him. He ate fruit. He drank water. He had very clean habits; no death wishes. As a survivor he had kept himself as healthy as a warrior with a spear. No cavities. Grew up in Idaho where the water had fluoride? No battle scars, disease, no wear or tear. She tore herself away from the memory of him which had become like a tangible object she could turn and view and study and reflect upon in her mind's eye.

In spite of being pregnant and wanting to send only the best messages to the forming life inside her, Mavis began to brew a resentment which turned to a desire for revenge. She began plotting against Jack as much as she had plotted with him. With the same intensity her anger brewed. She pictured sprinkling weed poison on his palm grove and took pleasure in imagining the expression on his face when he returned to see the yellowed, dead trees, trees he coddled and cared for and would return to while he ignored her, trees she was now jealous of; but Mavis feared his retaliation in the form of holding her face in his strong hands and looking right into her eyes to see if she were really capable of such a deed. She knew she could not take that look of disbelief when he knew by her eyes that she had done it. She would not have to say a word. He'd know, and his disappointment would stab her. He believed she was better than that. Could she really do it and withstand his judgment. She looked at labels in the weed poison section of the nurseries. So many and for so many different kinds of weeds. She read the small print to see what would kill palm trees. And then fled from the aisle where the smell of poison, of death-causing agents was strong. She was carrying life. How could she have her mind on killing. Jack's rejection of her was making her crazy. She consoled herself with slogans, "Better to have loved and lost than never to have loved at all." She tried not to let all the lost love clichés surface; but they did and now she knew their meanings. She thought of herself, before and after love. She was better after, for having loved. She remembered thinking while in the throes of love, "If I die now, I will have lived fully." Broken-hearted themes for logos coursed through her imagination, but each hateful image was shamed by the loyal voice reminding her to remember the love. "Separate it from him," the voice kept saying. "The love was you. Love is love. He was only a man. Protect what you felt. Don't deny it. Don't hate while you're pregnant. Be true to the love. Mavis plotted to leave her home, the place Jack would someday come sniffing around to see if she were still there, the spot where he had left her. Left, is right. And she vowed she would go away, fly to Florida maybe, somewhere where he could not find her. She knew it was only a test, this kind of thinking, to make Jack hunt her down if he really cared. He'd have to prove himself and if he failed the test, well, then, at least she wasn't just staying put and waiting for him to return. She revelled in the imagined expression on his face at his dismay to find she'd closed up her house and was *gone*. As gone and left as he was to her, she would be to him. And then that phase passed and she stayed and focussed on the pending birth of Jackie.

It would be a June baby. Mavis had almost forgotten the real Jack as the months went by and she focused on the baby, her work deadline, talking to her parents in Florida. A fantasy Jack remained. The impression of Jack. Her parents were ready to come out as soon as she gave the word and be there until the birth. She assured them she was fine. More than fine. Healthy as a horse and so was the baby. She sent them printouts of the the ultrasound. She scanned the ultrasounds onto her monitor and magnified them and marvelled and printed them out and hung them on the wall next to Jack's printouts. A girl.

She named her Jacquline and called her Jackie. Of course! She was big and growing bigger! A healthy girl. Sue came over to help. With Sue's coaching, Mavis learned to recite her lines if Jack ever called. "Jack who?" Sue came over daily in the ninth month and helped Mavis get by in her late pregnancy as she grew bigger and more awkward. She told Mavis how she had a glow about her she'd never seen before; and referred to "Jack Ass or Your Old Man, or What's-his-name, or whoever that guy was, the sperm donor, you say, ha, ha?"

Mavis remained silent, still loving the love she'd felt for Jack, whether she attached it to Jack or not. Jack had opened up a new world to her, how could she discount that. She wasn't the same person she'd been when she'd met him. "That's for sure," Sue joked, looking at the gigantic belly on Mavis, smirking, waiting to laugh out loud if she could catch Mavis' eye and share it with her. Mavis would not let go of remnants of her experience with Jack. She loved it all up to the point when he walked out. Details would surface and go right to the baby with a sharp pang when she was least aware of it. The picture show inside her head fed the fetus images of her father. Mavis felt that it was good; it was necessary. It was a fact.

"Yeah, right," Sue would quip, loading her voice with innuendo. Then Sue would cruise by the mango tree, with its thickening stalk and glistening leaves quivering in the breeze and snear, glancing comically at Mavis; "Have you watered this thing!" and laugh out loud. The once small palm had to be transplanted into a larger pot and sat beside the mango. "The three of you make quite a spectacle; here, let me take a picture; stand over there between the other seeds that Jack planted! Are you sure his name isn't Johnny Appleseed. He's left a trail of fertility passing through this town!"

In this way, Mavis passed the nine months. A lot of teasing from Sue, and a lot of support from her mother and father via the phone. They couldn't wait. Any longing for Jack had been replaced with physical discomfort. His image faded while the baby's became clear. The tiny hands and feet in the enlarged printouts of the ultrasound were studied for long moments while she rarely looked at Jack's pictures anymore. They had become fixtures, like the rest of her artwork. Just color and design, pattern, an assortment of logos, a finished work to hang and be seen with little emotional attachment to them; too familiar to take personally. The same month Mavis was due, the immature palm Jack planted sent out its first lacy birth of dozens of little pale dates that would probably never ripen, while the mango tree had pushed out a bud of sorts that looked like it was trying to bear fruit and having a test run at it. Bees had been cruising through her foliage all spring. When the pains started, Mavis decided not to call anyone. She grabbed her bag and got behind the wheel of her little car and drove herself to the hospital notifying her doctor. He would meet her there.

chapter ten

Jackie came into the world stoic and brave and with an uncanny awareness, looking around as if to assess where she was now, singling out Sue's presence. Sue shuffled, self-conscious, startled by the newborn's eyes turned on her. Mavis smiled at her "Little Jack" as she called Jackie at first. She began babbling in the postpartum state all that Jack had told her about himself as a baby. "Jack had the same black straight hair at birth and how it all fell out later and turned to gold... It's his nose and mouth, and look at her eyes. That's Jack. And how long the fingers and toes.

Ah...." She marvelled for a day under the hospital birthing room care, and then went home confident in mothering the tiny infant. Sue was awestruck and silent.

It's at the birth of this new life that the phone rang. Mavis was breast feeding.

Of course it was his voice. A simple,"Hello." She could see his Adam's apple move. The sound flooded her with memory, opening up those closed down places. It was him and she didn't say, "Jack who?" because he never said his name. Instead, Mavis said, "Jack?"

"Hi," he said. Adrenalin shot to her knees and elbows, through her heart and she began to hyperventilate. The baby startled. To calm herself, she took a deep breath and held it, attempting to stay with the old anger that had turned to an active indifference. She feigned wishing he had never called if that's all he could manage to say. Did he expect her to rejoice at the sound of his voice, ask a thousand questions to reveal how she suffered. She adjusted the baby over to the other breast, dropped the phone and the baby cried, a short squawk , over the disruption of her feeding.

Jack said, "What's that, new software?"

She said, "Yes, your daughter," and listened to the silence on his end. A long silence. And she was determined to remain silent on her end and let him be the one to break it. Her blood began to boil. She had Jack's attention now. It was his turn to *do* something, *say* something, clarify for himself what had transpired in his absence. Mavis would not offer any information after her initail response. She waited.

He said, "My daughter."

"Yes." That was it. He hemmed and hawed a bit and then she heard the dial tone. When she put the phone down she stared at the image in her mind's eye. Jack on the other end hanging up. What a strange reaction, although she knew he hated talking on the phone. He liked to read the face he was talking to. The baby came off the nipple and began to cry, sensing a change of focus in her mother. Mavis was brought back to reality; smiled and calmed the little one, assuring her that everything was okay.

"Yes, mommy had a fright. You're right little one. You know these things, don't you. Just like your daddy." Mavis closed her eyes, lay her head back, continued to breast feed as if the phone had never rung, yet she felt plugged into an electrical current. To steady herself, she chalked up Jack's reaction to being what Sue called him, "a jackass, indeed." Her friend was right afterall. Oh, well, she thought. I've gone without him through the worst of it; there's nothing to this, his sudden surfacing for a split second like the Loch Ness Monster. She chuckled and shook her head in mock calm and began to hum a lullaby. She didn't need Jack. One month of love making doesn't mean a thing after all to some men. But, for a woman, it can result in a lifelong miracle. He was simply a drifter and she had known that from the beginning. She drifted now, into a dreamy state with her baby, ignoring the buzz coursing through her body. A few days as a mother and her life had become dreamlike tending the baby, looking at the tiny face, wondering over the wonder of the world of the newborn. "Newborn" was a label on baby clothes she discovered at her baby shower. A whole world unto itself that she had never been aware of before and now immersed in as if baptised and coming up a new person. Baby Jackie let go of the nipple, fast asleep with her pink rosebud lips slightly parted, just the way Jack slept, and her tiny chest rising and falling rapidly with the little breaths. How fast the heart beats in infants she mused. How fast her heart was beating, too.

Mavis continued to sit on the deck, feet propped up on the railing, the two potted plants on either side of her wicker rocker, holding her precious bundle just looking at her and smiling over how the infant ate and slept, ate and slept. She would wake in a few minutes and feed again while Mavis held her at her left breast again. That one always filled first and fuller. It was slightly bigger. Jack had pampered the smaller one.

She'd always been amused by this. Now, she saved the smaller breast for the second feeding. Jackie's tiny face changed expressions; a tilt of an eyebrow, grimace of a mouth muscle. Mavis leaned back, closed her eyes, breast bared with baby attached again, when she heard footsteps at the side entrance, opened her eyes, and there he was. Like a magic show. First there is nothing and then his face is there above the gate. He is smiling, eyes intense, feasting himself on Mavis with the babe at her breast. It could be the title of a photograph with the look he shot at this scene.

"May I come in?" He waited for an answer. Mavis sighed, nodded. As light and swift as an Indian scout coming upon a deer with doe, he was knelt beside her on one knee, peered into the tiny face of his daughter, as if afraid to look at Mavis. He let her look upon him at first looking at the baby as the baby let go of the nipple and broke into her first smile or what seemed a smile. Was it gas pain? The timing was perfect. Jack grinned. Mavis couldn't help but smile.

Jack sat down on the deck at Mavis' feet, a tall man in the same posture in which she'd met him, his head lower than hers. He still could not hold her gaze, and only glanced to see her mood, rummaged in a pocket and brought out a little box and without a word, handed it to her. She took it, without a word, lifted the lid and saw a ring with a green stone lying on a square of velvet on top of cotton. It appeared to be an emerald surrounded by diamonds, or what appeared to be diamonds.

She looked down at Jack.

He said, "Will you be my wife?" Will you marry me?" Mavis laughed out loud, throwing back her head and resting it on the back of the rocker, exhaled and closed her eyes. The baby attached to the nipple again and began a vigorous sucking. Mavis' milk flowed so abundantly that it bubbled around the tiny mouth and spilled onto her little neck, soaking the newborn cotton t-shirt. While Jack waited for Mavis to say something, he touched the spilt milk on his daughter's neck with his naked finger and brought it to his own lips tasting it. Mavis shook her head back and forth. Nine months of silence and now this. Not one word or phone call. She closed the box, her heart pounding, continuing to shake her head.

"I can't," she said and held the box out to him. He did not lift his hand to take it.

"Do you have someone else?" he asked, swallowing audibly, his voice almost a whisper.

"Of course not," she snapped, this time pinning him with her eyes, taking Jackie off the breast, tenderly coddling her back to the crib, leaving her in the nursery to sleep. She stormed back to Jack. Her woman's voice rose, "You taught me what you learned as a child; don't get too close or you'll get hurt. Now, I've been hurt. I'm a different person than the one you left. You can't just walk back in and expect me to be the same." While she spoke, she buttoned up her bra from the front, pulled her t-shirt down and stood towering above him. "It's not that easy, Jack. You can't just walk back into my life. Didn't you learn that somewhere along the road?" She bordered on sarcasm, wanting to use his past against him, to wound him with all she knew about him; but fell silent. He'd obviously dropped in and out of nowhere all his life with people he knew, no doubt waved goodbye or simply disappeared and reappeared with a hello.

No one ever knew where he'd been or why he was back? He'd been a traveler, whimsical about relationships, loose in people's homes, using them as stopovers. He knew where they were, but they never knew where he was. And now he comes with a token of permanence.

Jack stands up, takes the tiny box from Mavis, lifts the top off, takes out the ring, very somber. He says, "Teach me. I can learn how to stay in one place." He looked pitiful and sincere, startding there in front of her like that. Her t-shirt shot hot with milk. He saw this, staring at the dampness; then took her hand, and she pulled away refusing to extend her ring finger as he tried to slip the ring in place. He pulled her to him and held her tight, forcing her to stay against his body. His shirt was soaked with milk.

Her heart went wild. Yes! she saw athletes on T.V. scoring points. Yes! But it wasn't about winning. How could she not be with Jack, forever. Yet, she shouted, "No!" to his earlier proposal. They heard Jackie let out a yelp and they went to her with Mavis blocking the way, so she alone, would reach the crib first. When she saw Jackie was all right, she led Jack back outdoors to the deck. "No! You can't ignore the fact that you left me. Why?" And the words trailed off as Mavis was overcome with grief and fury. In a streak of violence she threw herself on Jack's mighty chest with tooth and claw and tore at him in an attempt to destroy the very body and face she loved and now loathed, growing hot and wet herself with the effort to hurt him back. And he let her. When she was exhausted and his forearms were up to protect himself and his head tucked down, thwarting off her blows, hearing her struggle with his mass, making the same grunts and groans to reach him in hate as she made in love, she heard the most incredible reaction, chuckling. Jack was chuckling over her wrath. How dare he, and she found strength to claw at that laughing face one more time, leaving blood on his cheek when he least expected it. He'd let down his guard and she got in and tore flesh. It was what she wanted. This time he grabbed her wrists and stopped her in mid-flail at his face again. He held her away, and studied her face streaked with tears, runny nose, disheveled hair. She had messed herself up trying to beat him up with her smallness up against his largeness. He chuckled again and shook his head and said low and heavy, with Adam's apple bobbing, "Yes, I deserved that. You're right to want to kill me. Let me tell you why I ran away."

Mavis listened now, hunched into herself, not looking at Jack, still steaming with a need to see him hurt the way she had hurt for so long. Jack told her it scared him to know that she'd stolen his heart, that he didn't belong to himself anymore and he had to go test it. "I know I'm only half Indian, but a lot of my mother's ways were passed down to me, I guess. I didn't even know how influenced I'd been by her people. But, somehow, when I gave my heart to you, I gave my soul, too, and it scared me. All a man's got is who he is in the world, and when a woman comes along and steals away his heart, he doesn't know who he is any more. I ran. I was a coward. I had to see if it was true or not. If I stayed away from you, I'd see how much of a pull you had on me. If I kept staying away, I'd see how strong that pull was. I had to know, Honey." Mavis looked up. Was this a lot of blarney? She scrutinized Jack. A big guy like that being afraid of love. Really? she was thinking.

Jack continued, awkward, to tell her why he'd gone away and now came back. "I went back to the mountains of my childhood, you know, in Idaho, and climbed them, fasting. My Indian grandfather used to do that to get to know things, what to do. He'd find solitude and go without food, and come back down after a week or so or however long it took and would have some answers to what was bothering him. My mother told me this about her father. Remember I told you this?" Jack swallowed audibly again, a sign of intensity Mavis knew. Yet, she would not look up but buried herself, looking into her own lap, still seething.

"I couldn't get you out of my mind. The pull was so hard on me that I knew I'd left my heart here and I'd have to come back and get it some day. I had to test that? And I had to test you. I had to return to see if you'd be with someone else." Mavis shot Jack a look that could kill but Jack didn't drop dead. He chuckled instead, putting up one arm to shield his face in case she took a swipe at him. "I never got attached to a woman before. I never missed anybody before. I know you're the one. And once I knew that coming down out of the mountains, I knew I had to get a sum of money together, a job, to be equal to you. You know. I can't return as a drifter."

Jack tells how he went back to his old route driving cross country before his bid to drive the California coast came through; the late fall had been a wet one and he'd gotten into bad weather. It was on the news. He'd been in a truck wreck, no fault of his own. It was on T.V. Some mud slides. "It seemed as soon as I fell in love with you and let my guard down, I ran into a lot of trouble. I became vulnerable for the first time. I'd been going through life closed off to everything but plant life and then I was feeling all kinds of things. It was a distraction to be opened up. That mud slide came out of nowhere. In my old self, always ready for danger, I'd have sensed it coming; but after loving you and having you pulling on me from way out in California, I was distracted, always thinking of you."

Jack falls silent, takes a long look at Mavis' bent head. She can't look up. Not yet. He knows it will be awhile before she'll cool off. And he knows he's got all the time in the world, because he's where he wants to be, now. He talks to the top of her head, studying the multicolors of her mixed genealogy in the strands of hair in a turmoil springing from her scalp. She's a woman and he a man. He can handle this. Mavis is stilled and calmed again by Jack's presence. She believes his story. When her shoulders begin to shake and sobs roar from her throat, he knows she is his again. That she was only scared going it alone after loving him. He says, "You're as mad as a woman in love missing her man can get. I needed to see that. I needed to see that you didn't move beyond me and let some other man into your heart. I needed to see that you would be here and angry enough to slap me. And you did."

He chuckles again and Mavis sobs in throat-ripping torrents while Jack kneels and tries to hold her against him to comfort her. She stiffens and rocks with the anguish stored, for all those months. And then she stops, sniffs, blows her nose on the tail of her t-shirt, and sits wet-eyed and emptied out from having lost Jack. He was back. He tells her how he headed her way as soon as he got his California route and enough money together, wanting to surprise her. He knew there'd be a showdown.

He knew she'd be that kind of a woman. She was no

pushover. Yes, he'd grown a beard and had just shaved it off. That explained how pale his jaw was, in fact how pale he had become. He'd been in out of the sun, holding a job. He'd planned on getting the California coastal route and pulling into town every week and parking along the service road off the freeway and calling Mavis to come climb up into his cab where they'd make love. It was just a romantic vision, he admitted, picturing her parking her little car along the street behind his big rig, stepping up with his help pulling her in, and the sleeping compartment behind the driver's seat being a perfect nook for them.

Then, he'd see her on the way back. Mavis was drawn into this imaginary meeting, saw them cuddled in the truck's small quarters sharing the bunk for an hour or so. She would have loved that weekly love nest with him; but, knew now what had kept him away. While Jackie was incubating, Jack was also off in another world, to be born again and return to her.

Mavis looked at Jack. She pleaded with her eyes and shook her head, "Why couldn't you have told me all this? Why did you make me suffer not knowing, even beginning to hate you?"

"It doesn't work that way. If we had known, the test would have failed. We had to listen to our hearts. Our hearts had to tell us that we're supposed to be together. I know that sounds kind of silly coming from me, but that's the only way I could know how much I belonged to you and you to me. I could tell by the pain. It was painful for me too, the night I left, seeing you lying there sleeping, going off alone. I had to tear myself away. It wasn't easy; but I had to know if it was more than sexual passion. I knew I loved you when I missed your face, your words, the way you are. You're unique, Mavis. You're one of a kind. I've never met a woman like you before."

Mavis sighed. Is that what Indians do? Was this some kind of a tradition: fall in love, go off and test your survival skills, come back with wealth to set up the teepee with the waiting woman if she waited, too? A test for both of the love-crazed lovers? Come back with plenty of animal skins and furlined moccacins for a wedding gift, as well as beaded stuff? But, Jack did it whiteman style and brought back a bank account. She knew, now, that he had to do that for self-respect.

Wrung out and dry of tears, Mavis smiled at Jack, her eye-lashes still stuck together wet, put out her ring finger and said, "Yes." Weary and tired of not having Jack and now having him again put an end to her misery; but it would be a long while before joy would fill her heart. She would need time to learn to trust his love.

Together they stood and held each other and then ambled into the baby's room to gaze upon their creation. Jackie was smiling and looking up at them with her eyes wide open. Had she not slept through the whole commotion, but listened to the sounds her parents made getting back together?

In the late afternoon Mavis breathed away all her hurt and anger, running on the beach with Jack, to the pier and back, while Sue sat in the sand dunes with Jackie.

The sunset had a silver lining. How blantant could Mother Nature be.